TIMELY DEATH

TIMELY DEATH

SCOOTER REASER

Archway Publishing books may be ordered through booksellers or by contacting:

Archway Publishing
1663 Liberty Drive
Bloomington, IN 47403
www.archwaypublishing.com
1 (888) 242-5904

Cover designed by Tiger Eye Productions
Artwork by Scott DeDear

ScooterReaser.com
TimleyDeath.com

ISBN: 978-1-4808-2508-6 (sc)
ISBN: 978-1-4808-2509-3 (hc)
ISBN: 978-1-4808-2510-9 (e)

Library of Congress Control Number: 2015919536

Print information available on the last page.

Archway Publishing rev. date: 05/09/2016

ACKNOWLEDGMENTS

TO:
GREED,
without which there would be no Book

In memory of Mom and Dad

How easy it is to forget,
things that would not be,
if not for Mom and Dad loving me.

"For the love of money is the root of all evil; which while some coveted after, they have erred from the faith, and pierced themselves with many sorrows"

TIMOTHY 6:10

"To everything there is a season, and a time to every purpose under the heaven
A time to be born and a time to die
A time to kill; a time to weep and a time to laugh
A time to love and a time to hate; a time of war and a time of peace"

ECCLESIASTES 3

PROLOGUE

THE CROSSHAIRS OF HIS SCOPE WERE positioned perfectly on the podium where his target would appear in a few minutes. He was no sniper or trained killer, just a casual hunter with good marksmanship skills—abilities he hardly needed for this shot. His target was a mere two hundred yards from his concealed position and there were no security precautions in place. This was simply a Ladies Garden Society, a function to award a plaque to his target for a donation of some sort. This event was nothing political, no high value targets or attendees. Only a couple of wives of local politicians were there; the remainder was made up of those unable to come up with an acceptable excuse for not attending.

The situation was so impersonal and the cause so just that he knew he would have no remorse for the act. He would just pull the trigger and walk away. The rifle was untraceable and would be left behind. In the din and noise of the traffic below, it would be long after he was gone before anyone determined where the shot had come from. He had no apparent motive, did not know the target, had never met her or even seen her before; there would be no ties to him.

If not for his intervention, this event would not even make

the corner of the back page of the evening edition. Even with the incident, it would not make the front page and would be simply regarded as a random act of violence by some psycho.

The real motive would never be known but to a few like himself.

A limo pulled up near the curb, and his target emerged and went to stand next to the podium to be introduced. She was striking; even in the modest attire probably chosen to fit this occasion. She was a fox—Well—maybe some remorse.

Now she was standing absolutely still, with nothing between her and the rifle barrel. He centered the crosshairs on her bosom. He began to take up the slack in the trigger when he sensed someone else's presence nearby.

Without warning, something like a thin, steel wire slipped around his neck from behind. It was jerked tight as he pulled the trigger that fired the shot.

He was dead before the bullet struck the wall behind and to the side of his intended target.

One of two men who had just taken part in killing the shooter kicked the rifle out of the dead man's grasp,

"That was cutting it a little too close," John said. "We almost lost her this time."

"You're right," Tom nodded. "It seems funny we're trying to save her when soon we'll be trying to kill her."

"Yep," agreed John. "Timing is everything!"

CHAPTER ONE

AS I SAT AT THE ELBOW-WORN AND BEER-stained bar, I could not avoid noticing her as she sat erect on the faded blue café chair at a lavender table near the edge of the deck. She sat in the evening shade, taking in the last bit of the sun over the turquoise waters that lapped gently beneath her table.

It was then that she gave me the look. Not just a look, but *the* look—the one that made me glance around to be sure that it was intended for me.

Locks, the bartender (who was nicknamed after his long, unruly, unkempt dreadlocks) said, "Mon, dat look sure weren't fo' me, and if you's smart as some mons say, you know dat look ain't fo' you neither."

I couldn't deny the logic behind Locks's reasoning. After all, I was at least some years older than the woman and had the casual look and dress of an islander, even though I was a somewhat recent import to the region.

What would a woman like that possibly want with someone like me? It's not that I am too old or gray or that my linen suit is rumpled; it's just that I am not that lucky.

Oh well, I thought to myself as I left the bar and headed toward her table. *What else have I got to do this evening?*

"Nothing," I answered to myself, not realizing that I had spoken out loud.

"Nothing?" she said.

"What?" I paused. "Oh, sorry," I said. "I guess I just inadvertently summed up my plans for the future. I didn't mean for you to hear my thoughts."

"That is the most unusual pickup line I have ever heard," she said.

"It is?" I asked. "Am I being picked up?"

"That remains to be seen," she said. "Please sit down." She motioned to the well-worn chair across from her.

I did as ordered. "Ross Barr," I said. "Around here, I am known as Captain Barr or just plain Ross."

"I know," she said softly, not offering her own identity. She just sat there quietly, appraising what she saw.

In the silence that ensued, I did some appraising of my own. She was a little over thirty years old, very feminine, and fully developed. Her well-maintained and voluptuous body was packaged in a low-cut, high-class one-piece swimsuit with a long skirt cover-up that did nothing to cover up her long, unblemished legs, which were slightly tanned and obviously smooth to the touch. The warm, tropical breeze blew through her silky, brunette hair that she wore shoulder-length and loose. She had large, dark, evenly set eyes in a face that was not only beautiful, but exhibited *youth* and *maturity* simultaneously.

She was gorgeous, so gorgeous in fact that she had no

business giving me the look. Especially since I just noticed that she was wearing a plain, gold wedding band.

As I began to get up to leave, I said, "It has been nice meeting you, whoever you are; I'll just be in the way when your hubby shows up."

I assumed he would be a young, fit hunk or a rich, old codger; either way, it was time for me to go.

She placed her hand on mine and said, "Please, don't go." Her eyes caught mine and made the same request. "I am meeting no one. Perhaps I should have introduced myself sooner. I am Samantha Gail. Stormy, for short, and I am here alone."

"Does Stormy refer to your temperament?" I asked.

"No. Sam was already taken."

The sun blinked emerald green as it passed the horizon on its endless cycle.

"You obviously arrived on the cruise ship that docked across the lagoon on Victoria Island this morning," I said, knowing that no other vessels had arrived this week. "Very few tourists ever make it across the lagoon to this island," I informed her, "and even fewer come into this place."

This place, with its bar and restaurant with a *palapa* bar on the beach, also boasted a marina and several cabanas to rent to the occasional eco-tourist. It was nice but out of the way. The only way on or off the island was by the twice-a-day ferry or a private yacht. The small marina did a good business in season and there was a deep and well-protected anchorage which was usually full during the high season.

The island was named Elizabeth Isle after one of the queens of England; no one remembers which one and no one any longer cares. It suits my needs and current lifestyle. The fact that it was an unusually scenic and beautiful island was a bonus. The limited ingress and egress was another point in its favor.

"In fact, your ship should be leaving soon," I noted. "If you don't make it back and scan your identity card into its bowels of information, all hell will break loose and people will come looking for you."

"No one will be looking for me," she explained. "I bought a one-way ticket."

"What about the wedding ring?" I asked. "Is he comfortable with your absence?"

"What about yours?"

"Mine involves a long and intricate tale that is no longer relevant to my life and does not concern yours," I replied.

"Captain Barr, or Ross, as you prefer—I know those are not your given or birth names, and why you changed them is of no matter to me," she stated flatly. "I do, however," she continued, "know volumes about your former self."

"You think?" I stated more than asked.

"I not only *think,* I know. I know that you were a famous, highly successful, wealthy trial lawyer. You have a nationally renowned and beautiful wife and lovely kids—you had the American dream.

"I also know about your unexplained, if not discreet, departure from your life, friends, and family—and your practice," she said. "Much speculation was raised about the why and wherefore, but none of it ever suggested any malfeasance or negligence, much less anything conspiratorial or criminal. No reasonable reason for your dropping out," she concluded.

"First of all, lady," I said with a chill to my voice, "my life is none of your or anybody else's business, and while those may appear to be the facts, they are not the circumstances, and I have no intention of discussing them with you." I rose from the table. "Suffice to say, my situation is of my own making, and my exile is self-imposed and justly done," I finished.

Sensing a confrontation, she pushed herself back and softly raised her hand in a sign of peace. "Please forgive me if I seemed out of bounds," she said. "I don't care about your past except in the sense that you are highly qualified in an area of expertise in which I desperately need help."

"As you know, lady, I no longer practice law," I said.

"I don't need a lawyer; I need your tenacity. I also need your contacts as well as your current anonymity and lifestyle. Also, the fact that you are able, in a familiar and unobtrusive manner, to move throughout the islands is most important," she stated. "I need your services and money should be of no importance."

Before she could continue, I said, "Lady …" My voice grew a bit too loud for the occasion.

"Softly," she asked. "And please call me Stormy."

"Okay, Stormy, money is of no importance to me either; I do not want any; I do not need any."

"Good," she replied, "because I don't have access to any. I am, at the present, penniless. I cannot pay you for your services or your charter boat."

"What?"

"Please sit back down and give me a chance to beg. I am in a terrible fix. My life is in danger, and I have little time and no other options left," she pleaded. "I had to leave the ship in a hurry, and all I have is my purse, some makeup, and the clothes I am wearing."

I sat.

CHAPTER TWO

"I NEED TO HIDE OUT, TO BECOME INVISIBLE until we can determine the cause or circumstances that have brought me to this point. I know that this island is remote and unadvertised, but I was able to access it and there are those better able than I to discern its location and mine. I need to vanish," she continued. "You and your boat are ideal for my current needs."

"Lady --- uh, Stormy, my boat and I may or may not be ideal. Both of us are seaworthy; a little used perhaps," I stated.

"I am sure that I'll be more than satisfied with your services," she replied.

"Stormy—I am where you need me because I don't follow conventional paths. I acknowledge that a certain amount of society and civility are required for human intercourse and commonality is the benchmark by which we associate; however, I may not behave in the way you expect." I stated.

"I repeat—I am in a *desperate* situation and I do not even know what the situation involves or why I am in it, except that it has become apparent that my life is off the rails."

"And you know that, how?" I asked.

"I can't tell you except in vignettes of what has happened to me in the last several months. Things that involve me make no sense. Things happening to friends and peers make no sense," she mused.

"You know that most species hide from their predators by staying in the middle of the herd or school and acting like all the others," I offered.

"Do I look like all the others? I can tell you that I do not behave like the others."

"It's obvious that you wouldn't blend into a normal crowd, and I can only imagine how you behave."

"For that, you will have to wait. I'm sure I have only a few hours before my behavior will be severely restricted—or ended," she lamented.

I caught Locks's eye and motioned him over. "I assume *Sea Witch* is provisioned and topped off?"

"Mon, you be ready as da—oh, Lordy. You see dem fellas over der, Sir Boss? Dey don't belong on dis island."

"The ones that look like they should be attending a funeral for a wise guy?" I asked.

"Yea mon, dose."

Turning to Stormy I said, "Locks is right. Anyone can tell they don't belong here. They are either lost or looking for you. It looks like your hours have been cut to minutes and my explanation put on hold. It also appears that I have little choice when it comes to what to do with you."

I told Locks, "We need to go now and without being seen. Go over there and distract them so the lady and I can get out of here without being noticed."

"Si, Sir Boss."

"And quit calling me Sir Boss."

"Si."

"And forget you ever saw the lady."

"Hard thing to forget, but I do my best, Sir Boss."

CHAPTER THREE

AFTER AN EXIT BORN OF PURE STEALTH AND luck we made our way down the beach toward my place and *Sea Witch.* As we approached Stormy asked, "You mentioned something about seaworthy didn't you?"

I replied, "She's clean, sturdy, has great lines and, like you, just enough paint to bring out her beauty."

"Well maintained?"

"By my standards," I said.

"Will I be well maintained?"

"As long as you maintain your manners," I replied.

The dock ran along a bulkhead that faced the Atlantic but was protected by a large, natural reef that remained above water even at high tide. The older, exposed, fossilized part formed a barrier against the sea and, along with the living reef beneath, provided a habitat for the reef dwellers and a sanctuary for me.

Sea Witch was moored alongside, gently riding high on the incoming tide. She was a ketch motorsailer with her two masts smartly raked and taut against their stays as they pierced the moonlit sky.

Her dark blue hull and teak deck glowed faintly under the

three-quarter waxing moon that had risen several hours before sunset.

As we neared the dock a tall, well-built, handsome, dark-skinned man appeared out of the shadows on the deck. He wore a linen shirt with a lace-up neck tucked into almost knee-length cotton tan shorts with a blue webbed belt and a gold buckle. He had perfectly groomed and braided shoulder-length locks pulled tight and tied against the nape of his neck. He was the antithesis of Locks, even though they were cousins. He met us on the gangway.

"Sterling, may I present Ms. Stormy Gail, soon to be a fellow traveler of ours."

"My pleasure," replied Sterling in a British accent of which even Professor Higgins would have been proud. Sterling's accent, however, was not a matter of practice, but a matter of birth. Being born in the Queen's Islands and schooled on the Isle itself, his only acquired language was French, which he also spoke without a noticeable accent.

"Locks called and said to make ready to depart," Sterling explained. Gesturing across the bulkhead toward the yard and the large tropical-style house, Sterling said, "The staff will finish closing up *Casa Tango* and be gone by the time we are out of the channel."

"Casa what?" asked Stormy.

"I'll explain later," I replied.

"Well done, Sterling," I said. "We'll run northeast into and across the Gulf Stream with our navigation, spreader, and cabin lights on and under full sail. Once we exit the Gulf Stream on the east side, we'll take a heading to the south-southeast and kill all our lights, drop sails, and make way under auxiliary power for the remainder of the night. Our turn to the new course will coincide with the setting of the moon."

"Aye, aye, Captain," Sterling replied and he crisply ordered two crewmen, who materialized as if by magic, to cast off.

Sterling then went aft and took the helm.

I touched Stormy's elbow and asked, "Would you like to go below and freshen up? Your stateroom is the first one on port side- to your left."

"I know my port from my starboard as well as my aft from a—whatever," she said as she went below. "And I'll be back in two shakes. I want to be on deck as we leave."

"Terrific," I answered. "You have a lot of explaining to do."

CHAPTER FOUR

STORMY RETURNED TO THE DECK AND FOUND me forward of the main mast on the port side. *Sea Witch* was on a port tack, heeling just enough to make sitting and leaning against the cabin the best seat in the house. Elizabeth Isle, from which we had just departed, slipped by on our port side; twinkling lights dotted its black silhouette. The reflection of moonlight on the small waves made the silhouette appear to be set in diamonds. We moved almost noiselessly through the water, in rhythm with the sea. Our present heading provided a cool sea breeze across our deck.

Stormy sat beside me. We neither talked nor moved until the island dropped below the horizon.

She lifted her face up to me and I asked her, "Is this a good time for you to begin?"

"I don't know where to start," she said. "I'll tell you of my experiences over the past several months and see if you can figure out where it all began and perhaps even what it means."

She leaned back into my shoulder and looked out at the hills and valleys of the waves. But what she saw was her past.

"It was two or three months ago. I cannot be more precise because there was no singular event that marked a beginning," she narrated. "At first it was just a feeling that grew into shadowy encounters that I could never actually confirm. Then there were noticeable tails: the same people, same cars, furtive glances that seemed more than coincidences. About a month ago, I was nearly run down by a car while on a shopping trip. I was crossing at an intersection with the light, and was nearly across when a car swerved toward me. I had to jump out of its path and the driver sped off without stopping. At the time I put it off to nothing more than chance."

She went on, "A week or so later I decided to walk to a neighborhood restaurant near my beach house. Sometimes I take the car, but that night the weather was nice and I wanted the exercise. After having a few drinks and socializing with friends, I left and began walking back home. I had gotten about halfway back when a man, dressed mostly in black, came at me brandishing a knife. My first thought was that I was being mugged for my purse. I grabbed my keys out of the side pocket of my purse and threw my purse toward him, hoping that he would grab it and leave. He stepped right over it and kept coming toward me. I was terrified that he would rape me, and I turned and started running to my house. As I turned, I saw another man charging my direction from behind my attacker. Fearing now the horror of being attacked by not one but two men gave me the impetus to run faster than I thought possible.

"I kept running without looking back, and soon I could no longer hear their footsteps. I slowed a bit and looked back, and to my astonishment there was no one there. Both men had disappeared.

"I rapidly continued home, jammed the key in the door, let myself in and locked the door securely behind me.

"I picked up the phone to dial 911 and stopped. What would I tell the police? What had happened? Had I imagined it all? No; my purse! I had thrown it toward my first attacker. It must still be on the street. I sat down and tried to slow my racing pulse. After a moment I got up and went to the door. I wanted, I needed to look, to see, to confirm that this did indeed take place.

"I carefully chanced a peek out the door and there, on the steps, was my purse."

"Your what?" I asked out of surprise.

"My purse! Shall I continue?"

"Please do."

"I dumped all the contents out onto the console table near the door. Nothing was missing, nothing added. There was nothing to indicate that it had ever left my possession. By this time, I decided not to call the police. They would probably think I was a nut case.

"The final straw, as they say, came about ten days ago. I am a member of a foundation that promotes landscaping in public parks. I was scheduled to speak at a ceremony to honor past work by the foundation. Just as the introductions were starting, a shot rang out and a hole was blasted in the wall behind me."

"Was someone shooting at you?" I asked.

"I can't say. There were other people standing there with me. Many were the wives of local politicians."

"What did the police say?"

"That is the strange part. A man was found dead, his neck

broken, about a block away, along with the rifle that fired the shot. To my knowledge, the police department has taken no official or unofficial position concerning what took place."

I nodded and we were quiet for a moment. Her head grew heavy on my shoulder. It seemed that the anxiety and fear she had suffered, coupled with the ordeal of her recent travels, finally caught up with her and exhaustion won out. Her breathing took on a different rhythm, her grip on me eased, and soon she was fast asleep.

I carried her down to her berth and eased her on it. She rolled over on her side, facing the cabin wall, and continued to sleep soundly.

CHAPTER FIVE

THE MOON HAD JUST SET WHEN I RETURNED to the helm to help Sterling and the crew. We lowered all sails, extinguished all lights, started the twin auxiliary engines, and made our course change to the SSE, proceeding at a nice twelve knots. So rigged, *Sea Witch* became a force against the sea rather than a force of the sea.

One of the crew relieved Sterling at the helm, and we made our way to our staterooms to get some sleep before the coming day.

I awoke rested and made my way along the deck to the cockpit for morning coffee. The first hint of the new day was a fine line across an endless horizon that separated a calm sea from what would be a cloudless sky.

As I stepped down to the cockpit table behind the helm station, I saw Stormy leaning forward from her seat at the table, holding a mug of coffee. She sat, cross-legged, on her feet; her hair was wet and she was wrapped in one of the terry cloth robes we provide for our rare charter guests.

"Did you sleep well?" I asked.

"Better than I have a right to," she replied.

"We can join Sterling in a few minutes for an early breakfast, if you wish," I offered. "I didn't hear you get up, but I heard the steward banging pots around when I passed the galley."

"Excellent. I'm actually pretty hungry."

"Fine," I said. "Some clothes will be sent to your cabin. They should fit well enough until I can take you ashore for something more befitting your style and temperament. Meet us in the dining salon in about fifteen minutes, OK?"

"OK," she said as she tried to walk back to her quarters without tripping on the oversized robe.

When she entered the dining salon, Sterling and I rose. Sterling pulled out her chair and seated her at the head of the rectangular table. He and I sat at either side. The leaves had been removed so it would only seat six, rather than the ten that it could easily accommodate.

She had chosen, from the limited clothing selection, a pair of cuffed, khaki shorts and a white-collared, long-sleeved shirt with the sleeves rolled up just above her elbows. She had knotted the shirt tail, in front, just below her breasts. She could not have looked better if she had worn a custom-designed ensemble.

At the wall beyond the end of our table was a large flat screen HD television that raised and lowered from a cabinet built just for that purpose. It was raised and a news channel was on. Due to the early hour and our location, we were several hours ahead of the East Coast and the announcer was merely repeating last night's news.

Stormy asked, "What's for breakfast? I'm famished."

"Anything from Eggs Benedict to Huevos Rancheros," I answered.

"Wow," she said and gave the steward an order for a more common breakfast item, consisting of eggs over easy and bacon.

"I had no idea your boat was so large and so—so, elegant."

Boat? I thought. "Uh, thanks," I said.

"And all the electric gizmos and stuff—they're everywhere! I have never seen so many ropes and cables and pulley things. I mean, I know about sailboats and I have even been on one before, but this is overwhelming. And yet nothing seems cluttered or out of place."

I had no reply.

Sterling, thank God, offered to elucidate. Sterling was the one responsible for seeing that the design on which we had collaborated was carried out at the yard. He lived near the yard for most of the two years it took to build *Sea Witch.*

"*Sea Witch,*" he began with pride, "has the latest navigation and communication equipment available to date. In addition to a unique hull design, she is operated almost entirely by computer driven hydraulic and electrical systems. This is why we need so few crew members."

"Oh. Are you also responsible for the exquisite woodwork, furnishings, and décor?" Stormy asked Sterling.

"Even the china and the silver service," I interjected.

"Of course there were two European design firms that also participated. They implemented Ross's grand design and I saw to its completion," Sterling added.

"What was Ross's grand design?" asked Stormy.

"He wanted the ambience of a private naval club of 19th century England," Sterling explained with a satisfied smile.

"You mean those stuffy old clubs where women were not

allowed and the men sat around on overstuffed chairs and smoked cigars and drank brandy?"

"Precisely," answered Sterling. "You have, no doubt, noticed the dark walls with intricate paneling, inset with original oils of a nautical nature?"

"I have."

"You may not recognize that the wood is African hardwood, similar to mahogany, but it has a pommele or dappled grain which in this case has been richly fitted and finished by some of the best wood workers on the planet. All this is set off with raised panels, intricate crown molding and baseboards, and hand fitted tongue and groove walnut flooring.

"All the furniture was custom-made at the shipyard using only the best fabrics and leathers available, and each was chosen by the decorators to compliment the specific room it was designed for."

"Is that real granite in my bathroom?" asked Stormy.

"Your head—not bathroom," Sterling corrected kindly. "Granite, marble, onyx, and Venetian tile adorn the surfaces in yours and all the heads and counters onboard. The galley, notwithstanding, is stainless steel and rivals the best commercial kitchens on land.

"Furthermore, *Sea Witch* makes 3600 gallons of fresh water out of sea water daily and, when needed, can produce enough electricity to power six average suburban homes," he continued.

"What does Ross's office look like? Is it all a mess or is it nice and neat?" asked Stormy.

"Perhaps you all have forgotten, I am still here," chimed Ross.

Ignoring Ross and Stormy's question, Sterling went on with his description. "His office is a little different. It is paneled with hard woods salvaged from sailing ships. His desk is from the *HMS Clayton* an old whaling vessel, and his tables and credenzas are from its hatch covers. The furnishings are covered in fine grain leather, tufted and stained oxblood."

"Is that all?" teased Stormy.

"No, but enough for now. I promise you a tour when time permits. There is one more thing—*Sea Witch* can move all of this and us anywhere in the world there is water."

When he finished with his explanation, Sterling began mindlessly surfing the news channels as a new hour began on the East Coast.

CHAPTER SIX

"STOP!" STORMY ORDERED. "I MEAN, GO back," she said to Sterling, "to that channel with the item about Devane."

Unsure what item she wanted, he handed her the remote.

She located the channel just as the newscaster said, "...also we have just received additional information about the late evening shooting in Los Angeles. Apparently there were a total of six people shot and presumably killed. Only one name has been released and that is of Alfred J. Devane III, who resided in Los Angeles. The other five names are being withheld pending notification of family. What authorities tell us is that all six were leaving a charitable fundraising event at the museum. There were ten or more persons waiting for their transportation to arrive when the shooting began. The shots were fired from one or more locations concealed near the crowd. All six were shot within seconds of each other."

"Dear God!" Stormy exclaimed, "Alfie, he was a childhood friend of my husband's and a dear friend of mine. What is happening? What is going on?" she moaned.

"Stormy!" I said, raising my voice in order to get her

attention, "Do you think this is related to what's been happening to you?"

"I don't know. I don't know. I just do not know."

I took the remote from her and turned off the television. "Let's finish breakfast," I said, "and later, when more information is available, we may better understand what's happening. One thing I do know is that I had better keep you sequestered," I added.

"It's a good thing I know what sequestered means," she said in an attempt at levity.

CHAPTER SEVEN

BREAKFAST EATEN, DISHES CLEARED, COFFEE served, Stormy and I sat alone at the table.

"Stormy," I began, "I am not without resources and they are being used as we speak to uncover the mystery surrounding these incidents."

"I know."

"You know?"

"I mean I know you are not without resources and that you have capabilities well beyond what you profess. I didn't know that you were already working on my problem and for that I thank you; actually, I am extremely grateful."

"You're welcome," I said, "In a few hours we will know all there is to learn. Until then, perhaps you can humor me by telling me something about yourself."

"Long version or short version?" she asked.

"Only the pertinent parts; plus, all the juicy bits."

"Wouldn't be the short version then," she winked. "I was a small town girl. Moved to the big city, went to college, got a job with a big corporation—the usual."

"I bet not too usual."

"I will admit that I was inducted into the "country club" set from the start. I moved up the social ranks early and quickly.

"Don't get the wrong idea," she warned, "I did not sleep around. My social and business contacts were just that: social or business. Married couples formed the majority of my friends, and they crossed over to the highest levels of the corporate world."

"Any marriages or affairs badly ended?" I asked. "Disgruntled heirs or business deals gone south?"

"A few affairs—all nicely and amicably concluded --- eventually. One possible exception, but other circumstances intervened to end it.

"One marriage," she paused and took on a sad, pensive look; then smiled and repeated, "One marriage."

"Am I getting too personal?" I asked.

"Yes," she said, "but it was a wonderful time of my life and is still a pleasant memory. I would be happy to share some of it with you."

"As much or as little as you wish."

"He was older. The difference in our ages was greater than the difference between mine and yours. He was a widower. His only wife died at a young age and they had no children. He lived alone for many years and we met both socially and for business purposes. We were comfortable together and everyone began to think of us as a couple. One day we just decided that marriage would be good for both of us."

"Sounds a little too matter-of-fact to me," I noted.

"I could not say it was a wild, passionate love affair. It was a lovely warm marriage with passion enough. It was loads of fun and we were also best friends."

"What happened, may I ask?"

"It ended unexpectedly, over two years ago, due to a rare and all pervasive, totally untreatable cancer. We had been married a little over five years before its onset and diagnosis. The time we had left was measured in weeks. There was hardly time to dwell upon it."

"Was there time to prepare? I am not trying to be insensitive and I apologize if I seem to be. What I am getting at is: Were there any loose ends that might play a role in your present circumstances?"

"I don't think so. He had no children and we had none together."

"No heirs other than you?" I asked.

"Yes. No. I mean, there are other heirs. His brother, my husband's only sibling, had two boys. I say *had* because his brother predeceased him. We spent very little time with the boys, however. They have their own lives to live and, of course, they are younger and we had a different set of friends. We were always very cordial and had a good relationship with them. I still see them at parties and events and we keep in touch."

"Were they taken care of in your husband's will?" I asked, sorry to be so blunt.

"No. However, they were very well taken care of in their father's will. I was the sole devisee of my husband's estate and they got nothing. But, as part of the estate plan, at my death his nephews inherit whatever I own at the time of my death."

"Do they fear that you may dispose of the assets before your death? You are still young and may live a long time. Or are they, perhaps, not willing to wait?"

"Neither, I believe. First, they are very wealthy in their own rights and, secondly, there is no way I will leave this world with less than I have now."

"I don't understand."

"I have not been completely candid with you. It is true that at the moment I am without funds. The reason, however, is that I have no way to access my accounts without revealing my whereabouts."

"That part I understand. It's the part about having more assets later than now. What, do you not eat?" I mused.

"No, silly. I didn't want to have to admit this to you, but my husband left me as one of the richest women in the world."

CHAPTER EIGHT

AFTER A LONG PAUSE AND A SIGH, I responded sternly, "Come with me, let's go up top for a stroll around the deck."

"Why?" she asked teasingly. "Have I upset you? Are you going to throw me overboard or make me walk the plank?"

"No," I chuckled, "I just should have realized who you were before now, Mrs. Samantha Gail Richter. Or Mrs. Samuel L. Richter, Jr. I met Sam years ago, before you were in the picture."

"This is not going to make a difference, is it?" she pleaded, "I mean, with you helping me?"

"No."

As we walked along the deck, the morning was taking full shape and promised a kind and benevolent sea for our rush to safe harbor.

"Are you going to ask me why I didn't just hire bodyguards and security to protect me and not bother you?"

"No."

"No?"

"No."

"Why not?" she asked.

"Because, I know why. Bodyguards would not insure your safety. They would offer you at best a false sense of security and a very restricted life style. Even the Secret Service hasn't been overly successful in protecting their charges." I continued, "A great author had his protagonist reply to the question of what could be done if one's life was threatened. The reply was, 'Quit licking stamps.'

"I give you credit for knowing that you must cure the problem, not just treat the symptoms," I concluded.

"They said you were intelligent," she replied.

"They?"

"Yes—those mutual friends of ours who insisted you were my only hope."

"Ah, yes, those nameless ones who know I have a weakness for damsels in distress," I suggested.

She chuckled.

"While you were eating breakfast, Sterling had one of the crew move you to one of the VIP suites—it looks like you'll be with us for a while."

She reached out and squeezed my hand, and then stepped directly in front of me. She lifted her chin, fixed those translucent brown eyes on mine and said softly, "I will never be able to repay you for what you are doing for me."

I met her gaze and replied, "I do not ask nor expect you to."

We faced the deep indigo blue sea. As the waves rolled past I could sense her closeness to me and smell her presence—a trace of Cartier, perhaps. No. Just the essence of a woman, but more acute with her than most. We continued to stand by the rail, each wrapped in our own thoughts.

I broke the silence. "By tonight we will anchor off an island populated by relatives and friends of Sterling and the crew. Our ingress and egress will go unreported. We'll provision for an extended voyage, and you'll be able to buy the things you need for yourself.

"You can take the first boat in and roam the island freely—Sterling will make sure you get the last boat out. Anything you want will be put on *Sea Witch*'s account and brought on board for you. Use this opportunity to enjoy the beach, because we may not be on dry land for some time."

"What are you going to do while I am ashore? Are you going to do some sleuthing or just take a nap?" she joked.

"Not that it is any of your business, but I need to meet Sterling in my office. Please make yourself comfortable until we anchor and be ready to go ashore. One of the stewards will provide you with whatever you need. I'll see you before you disembark."

"Aye, Aye, Capt. Bligh." She teased.

I left her at the rail, watching a frigate bird circling a likely lunch, and went to my office via a companionway that bypassed my cabin.

Sterling was waiting for me. A stack of papers lay on the mahogany table in front of him,

I pulled up a club chair rather than taking a seat behind my desk.

"What have we gathered from our allies and abettors?" I asked as I leaned over for a look.

"More than expected," he replied. "Our people checked anything and everything similar to the recent occurrences and a pattern seems to be emerging."

"How so?"

"The six shootings in L.A. all involved persons in a list published as the five hundred wealthiest Americans and generally referred to as *The List*. The one exception was a bodyguard that was apparently not a target, but was in the line of fire either by accident or in his line of duty.

"Most interesting is the fact that other people on *The List* have been murdered in the three months before Stormy's arrival. The common thread between the killings is that no motive has been discovered for any of them—all have been killed by muggers or snipers, and all have been killed within the previous ninety days even though not a single murder from that prestigious list has occurred for years, at least none unsolved. None of the muggers or the snipers has been found or identified, save for one found with his neck broken, and in the case of the snipers all of the weapons used were left at the scenes and were untraceable. In the L.A. shootings, the one in which Stormy's friend Alfie was killed, the L.A.P.D. determined that two snipers were involved."

"Are our sources getting complete and accurate data?"

"Absolutely! We have a complete overview that I doubt the various local law enforcement agencies have obtained as yet. Should we clue them in?" he asked.

"Not yet," I replied. "We don't want to alert the killers that we're on to them, and anything we give to the local authorities will, most certainly, be leaked or made public in press releases. We need to have some advantage, however small."

"So how does all of this play into Stormy's situation?" asked Sterling.

"I am not sure. What do you think?" I asked.

"She meets most of the criteria. No attempt before three months ago. Mugger or muggers/snipers. However, I don't believe she is on *The List*_even though Sam was on *The List*. Nonetheless there is one major disconnect," he said.

"What is that?" I asked.

"She is not dead!"

CHAPTER NINE

"NONE OF THE OTHER VICTIMS HAD unsuccessful attempts on their lives—they all appear to have been killed without incident. Yet Stormy escaped all three attempts on her life. One through actions of her own, but the other two seem more than fortuitous. The mysterious disappearance of her knife-wielding attacker and the dead sniper are inexplicable," Sterling said.

"There has to be an explanation. We just don't have enough information to piece the puzzle together," I insisted.

Sterling nodded. "True. Perhaps she really is in no danger. But I fear she is."

"Through circumstances I can't explain, she has placed herself in our care. I assumed the responsibility. There is a legal precedent that states that one has no duty to throw a drowning man a rope; but, once the rope is thrown, all due care must be used to pull the man in," I replied.

"What about a drowning woman?" asked Sterling.

"Are you implying that ...?"

"Well, do you care to answer?"

"If you are asking if I would do this for just anyone, the answer is NO. I am doing this only for Stormy and for reasons I do not understand," I admitted. "Nonetheless, the principle still holds. We must conduct ourselves as if her life is in great peril."

"I agree." Sterling gathered the paperwork from the table. "Do we have a plan?"

"Yes, Plan A."

"Plan A?"

"To keep her alive until we come up with Plan B."

"That is a good plan," Sterling said as he exited the office.

CHAPTER TEN

ALTHOUGH STERLING AND I EACH HELD Masters papers, I kept a live-aboard Captain on *Sea Witch* at all times. The Captain was capable of navigating the channel we were about to enter, but Sterling had made this passage many times and knew the route through the narrow twisting shoals better than most. Sterling personally took the helm as we approached the narrow unmarked channel on the lee side of the island. In order to avoid the shoals, Sterling had to read the water. The deep blue of the Atlantic became a brilliant turquoise of many hues as we entered the narrow waterway, and each vibrant color told something about the conditions of the sea and aided Sterling in his navigation of the difficult passage.

Stormy stood on the bow sprit, absorbing the scene as we passed through mangroves, palms, and a myriad of other vegetation on our way. We broke out into the bight, which was a small clear body of water that stretched the length of half a mile from shore to shore. The shore was actually fine coral, pink in color; the entire shoreline appeared as one bright pink oval surrounded by thick endless flora.

There was no pier or quay, and we anchored several hundred

yards from the beach close to the nearest large clearing, which contained a dozen or so buildings.

Stormy walked to where I stood, near one of the tenders that was being readied for launch.

"Why are the crew dropping anchors off the front … uh, bow and stern?" asked Stormy.

"To keep *Sea Witch* from swinging about with the tide. And to steady her for loading and unloading our provisions and personnel."

Sterling joined us, shouting orders to some of the crew.

"How can such a small harbor provide an entire island with the supplies needed?" she asked.

"I will defer to Sterling—he was born on this island," I nodded in his direction.

She turned to Sterling, who explained that the island was named Saint Catherine but was actually known as St. Cats to its inhabitants and most of the other islanders in this part of the West Indies.

"It is much larger than you would expect from this," he gestured to the small bight. "We came here to avoid detection. There is a large proper harbor on the southeast side that provides our lines of communication with the rest of the world. There is even a small airport with daily scheduled flights. The major town is St. George; it has a population of several thousand. And there are many towns and villages spread around the island. The small bight we are in—"

"What is a bight?" Stormy interrupted.

"It is a body of water with only one ingress or egress. This particular one was once used by rum smugglers to hide from the authorities. Its hidden location suits our purpose well.

"Here, our launch is ready. Are you coming with us, Ross?" asked Sterling.

"No thanks, I need to do some research and make some calls," I bowed slightly. "With your permission, I will meet you all ashore later."

CHAPTER ELEVEN

STERLING AND STORMY BOARDED THE tender for the short trip ashore. She stood in the bow and braced herself as the crewman beached the tender on the pink-sanded shore. Another crewman helped her over the side and into the shallow surf.

Stormy waded ashore through the surf and up the beach in her bare feet as Sterling came ashore just behind her. "Good show," he said, and pointed to an old pickup truck that had just arrived alongside the beach. It was brightly painted and occupied by a strikingly beautiful and brightly dressed young woman, near Sterling in age.

The woman threw herself out of the truck and ran down the beach, leaping into Sterling's arms. After they concluded their passionate embrace, all three walked to the pickup truck.

"Ms. Stormy, I would like to introduce you to Mrs. Linda Loraine Stanford, my wife."

"Sterling?".

Guessing the question, he stated, "Sterling is my given name; Stanford is my surname."

"A pleasure to meet you," said Stormy, offering her hand. They shook.

"I will be your guide while you're here with us," Linda related with the accent of a California transplant.

"Go, ladies, and do your whatever you women do; I have work to do. Let's meet later for supper," suggested Sterling.

Linda, still holding Stormy's hand, pulled her toward the waiting pickup. Once inside, they drove up a coral road that led from the beach to a picturesque village with a wide central avenue and many intersecting streets.

Stormy gushed, "I had not expected such a bustling and beautiful town in the mists of this tropical foliage,"

"There are several towns and villages similar to this one, some larger and some smaller. And there is St. George, which is cosmopolitan and very much like any of the small coastal towns in America along the east coast," Linda explained. "I have been instructed by my dear husband to take you shopping, and I am told we have *carte blanche*. Let's get to it!"

After several enjoyable hours of assembling a wardrobe of lightweight, colorful tropical outfits, Linda and Stormy entered a restaurant and lounge for a rest and *aperitifs* as Linda put it. Linda ordered in a fluent French that impressed Stormy to no end.

"How long have you known Ross?" she asked in a serious tone, once the waiter had left.

"Several days," Stormy replied.

"Several days?" she repeated with surprise, and became silent.

Their order arrived. It consisted of French champagne, and Russian caviar, and the appropriate accompaniments, along with an assortment of tea cakes and sweets. The waiter withdrew and, as he did so, Stormy broke the silence. "Yes, I knew of him but he and I had never before met."

"Sterling gave me a condensed account of your plight and Ross's desire to aid you, but I presumed your acquaintance was substantial … Ross is not a man to, to, shall we say, come out of his "*querencia*" for just any one person or thing."

"I was told that he was reclusive," Stormy replied.

"You were correctly told. He trusts my husband, but they go way back—even I do not know how they first met."

"Have you known Ross long?" Stormy fished.

"Not really. I met Sterling in D.C., where I was working for the U.N. I'd just moved there from California, and had few friends. Sterling is and was a consular *charge de affairs* for the Saint Catherine Protectorate. We met at a diplomatic party hosted by Ross."

Stormy smiled as Linda sighed theatrically.

"It was the old cliché for Sterling and I—love at first sight. We have been together for six years and married for four."

"How long has Ross been in the West Indies?"

"Ever since he became a recluse. Before Sterling and I met."

"Do you have any idea why—?"

"No, I know Sterling does," Linda interrupted. "But it is a taboo subject and I respect that."

"I'm sorry, I shouldn't pry into his past," Stormy backpedaled. "I'm certainly thankful for his interest in my problems. And for yours and your husband's concern, also."

"Come along, Stormy," Linda cheerfully directed. "We have a bit more shopping to do before we meet the men for supper."

Sensing that her opportunity to learn more about Ross had ended, Stormy willingly followed her new friend.

Throughout their shopping spree they left each establishment without being presented with or settling the bill, a practice to which Stormy became accustomed.

The women continued shopping until Stormy had assembled enough pieces to maintain her wardrobe for several weeks. "Do you think I have selected items appropriate for the occasions we are likely to encounter?" she asked Linda, finally, continuing with a blush—"Do you think that Ross will like them?"

"Honey, the only interest Ross will have in your dress is how long it will take him to get you out of it." She laughed.

CHAPTER TWELVE

THE *MAÎTRE D'* ESCORTED LINDA AND STORMY through a private entrance into the posh private dining room of the St. Charles Hotel on the outskirts of St. George. It overlooked the Caribbean Sea through a large glass window on the seaward side.

Rich paneling, lit mostly by candles, surrounded a series of white-clothed tables. Sterling and I were seated at a table for four near the window. We rose to seat the ladies. The table was set with china, silver and crystal, but the surrounding tables lay bare. It was obvious that we were to have the dining room to ourselves.

"You look absolutely stunning tonight," I exclaimed and took Stormy's offered hand in mine. My eyes played over her again and again. I lacked the will to stop staring at her.

She nodded pleasantly and I released her hand and pulled out a chair, seated her, and returned to my seat without shifting my gaze from her eyes.

"Ross," called Linda, who was already seated.

"Yes," I answered without turning.

"Do you like Stormy's dress?"

"Absolutely! She looks beautiful."

"I asked if you liked Stormy's dress," repeated Linda.

"Oh yes, your dress is fine. Uh, I love it."

"Good, you paid for it," Linda joked.

Sterling interposed, "I hate to interrupt, but I should mention that we have changed our departure date, Stormy. We need the light of day to navigate the channel out of the bight—preferably between the hours of ten a.m. and four p.m., with clear skies. Tomorrow is forecast to be mostly cloudy, along with a forty percent chance of thunderstorms. It is not possible to read the water under those circumstances. Therefore, we can't depart until the day after tomorrow at the earliest."

"Because of our forced delay, Linda and Sterling have graciously invited us to stay with them," I added.

"Yes," Linda chimed in. "It will be fun."

"That would be good fun," Stormy said, nodding. "And another day ashore would be welcome." She blinked suddenly, as if in doubt.

"They have a grand six-bedroom villa," I reassured her. "I am sure you will find a room that suits you." Stormy nodded, clearly relieved. Then I continued. "With that bit of business out of the way, I wish to invoke the "The Rule"."

"What rule is that?" asked Stormy.

"Ross doesn't allow any talk about business or personal issues at dinner," answered Linda.

"Yes, I've wasted many a wonderful meal with matters that could best be faced at other times and places. Civility should prevail during dinner, if nowhere else."

At that, the appetizers began to arrive, and Sterling began his commentary on the coming dinner.

"St. Cat was an English Colony that gained some autonomy and became a protectorate of Great Britain. This occurred during one of the many times that European nations traded Caribbean Islands back and forth as reparations for wars and other reasons that had no relevance to or consideration of the islands populace. As such, our customs and cuisine remain English, although our closest island neighbors are French. Over the years, we have exchanged customs and cuisine with the French, as well. Also, we are Caribbean. I point this out to illustrate the background from which our fare, this night, originates."

At that, several waiters appeared and a large serving platter was placed mid-table.

Sterling began, "The first offering consists of locally caught seafood. A cold combination including salt water crawfish, yellow tail snapper, yellow fin tuna, spiny sea urchin, and squid."

One of the waiters retrieved the platter and another began to serve the seafood cocktail. He placed small portions on plates that had been exchanged for our charger plates. The fish had been seared before being sliced and the lobster tail broiled; the sea urchin and squid had been sautéed. A lightly flavored remoulade sauce had been drizzled over it all.

The head waiter offered *Bon appetite* and we began.

Next we were served cups of conch chowder with oyster crackers.

"Conch is a staple among the peoples of the Caribbean," Sterling said. "Before the advent of cheap, refrigerated shipping, conch provided nearly thirty percent of our daily protein.

It can be prepared in a soup or salad, made into conch fritters, fried, sautéed, or served raw with lime juice."

Stormy ate the chowder with relish, savoring each spoonful.

"Now we will cross the pond," Sterling gestured, "and have slow roasted prime rib of beef, bone in, accompanied by peas and mash. Oh, and of course, *au jus* and horseradish."

Each portion of beef was cut to order at tableside, plated with the sides, and served.

After we finished the main course, Sterling elucidated further.

"I will spare you the traditional British dessert of cheese and biscuits, and instead we shall have *crème brûlée*. The desert, along with the wines, constitutes the French portion of our dinner."

We ate the *crème brûlée* as we had most of the meal, accompanied by light-hearted conversation and with no mention of the circumstances that had brought us together. After the table had been cleared, Stormy said, "I must admit that was one of the finest meals I have had the pleasure of consuming. The incredible part was the wine to which you so casually referred. I have attended many high-end wine tastings and there have been only two occasions on which I have had a Bordeaux from one of the first five growths. This place must have some wine cellar," she expounded.

"Actually, these bottles were brought ashore from *Sea Witch*'s cellar," Sterling informed with a smug grin.

Stormy looked at me and asked, "You realize what you served tonight?"

"Certainly," I casually replied, "a turn of the century Chateaux Margaux. We have the others as well."

"You mean the Lafite-Rothschild, Latour, and the Haut-Brion?"

"And the Mouton-Rothschild. All prior to 1959," I affirmed.

"Not to mention the Chateau d'Yquem we had with dessert."

"Ah, yes, the Premier Cru Superieur," I allowed.

"That's the one that Thomas Jefferson declared the best wine of France?" Stormy asked.

"True; but that was before the 'noble rot' was made part of the process. The 'rot' requires up to twelve different harvests of the vineyard to assure the grapes are picked at precisely the correct degree of ripeness," I pointed out.

"I heard that the sauternes can be racked for a century or more."

"Perhaps. A wine expert named Robert Parker supposedly scored an 1811 vintage at one-hundred points when it was opened in 1996."

"And you down played the entire wine service. Was this some cheap trick to determine my bono fides—you know, like the princess and the pea? Shame on you."

"Not cheap," I replied.

"*Touché*."

"Let's have brandy and espresso at the house," requested Linda in the somewhat awkward silence that followed. With that we prepared to leave.

The *maître d'* then approached and whispered in my ear.

"There is a gentleman here to see you, sir," he said, handing me a note and pointing down the hallway to the adjoining lounge. "He's says it's quite urgent ..."

"What is it?" Stormy asked. I looked at the note in my hands, not yet willing to see what it held.

"Probably nothing," I answered. "Why don't you and Linda take the town car to the villa—a driver awaits you. Sterling and I have a matter to attend to, but we will be along shortly."

"Does it concern me?" Stormy asked meekly.

"It won't when we're through dealing with it. Do not worry yourself—trust me to take care of this," I stated flatly.

That seemed to suit Stormy just fine. "Thank you," she said warmly. "I know that I can trust you with my life."

At that, Linda and Stormy left, arm in arm.

Not long after, the two women sat in a drawing room on the first floor of *Villa Mar.* Compared to the great room, the drawing room was all about comfort. Cushions, fabrics, deep upholstered club chairs, ottomans, and handy tables for all manner of things were pleasingly arranged throughout the room. Neither woman discussed Stormy's present situation. Instead, they continued the banter that had begun at dinner.

"You refuse to tell me anything about Ross, so tell me about yourself and Sterling, please?" Stormy asked expectantly.

Studying Stormy for a moment, Linda shook her head and said, "Alright, it can't hurt."

"I had a very normal, simple Southern California upbringing. I have a mom, dad and an older brother and sister, all doing well back in L.A." I went to UCLA, got my Masters and went to work at the U.N. and met Sterling."

"What about Sterling?"

"Sterling is a fifth generation islander. His family became influential at the beginning of the 19th century when Europe began loosening its hold on the Caribbean and allowing local rule. Sterling's grandfather was and his father is, the Governor-General for the entire Saint Catherine protectorate and Sterling is in charge of all commercial development."

"Really!" Stormy exclaimed.

"Really," Linda repeated, "Someday I'll take you over to meet my in-laws and we'll have lunch at the Governor's Mansion."

"How did Sterling and Ross meet?" Stormy asked, hoping to keep Linda talking and gain some information about Ross.

"Neither of them will talk much about that time in their lives. From the bits and pieces I have learned, they met soon after each had finished their grad studies. They were apparently recruited into some type of quasi-governmental organization and spent several years working together."

"Doing what?"

"If you can find the answer to that, you'll know more than I."

Their eyelids began to droop, "I would like to stay up until our guys get home," said Linda sleepily.

"So would I, but I can hardly keep my eyes open either," Stormy answered. "Why don't we call it a night?"

The ladies retired to their respective rooms. Stormy found her purchases neatly hung, and the king-sized bed was turned down and ready.

As she lay in the big bed and nestled into the down pillows, Stormy began to relax and replay the last few days, which had transpired so rapidly that she had been robbed of the time to think of Ross. Now, safe and secure in the bed, Stormy remembered his eyes on her at dinner.

His hair was somewhat long, wavy, and well-styled—brown with hints of grey and sun bleached strands intermingling. He had striking yet soft features and probing, sensitive eyes. He was broad shouldered with a statuesque frame and stood a little over six feet tall.

He was handsome, no doubt. But more than that he was confident, worldly, at ease in any situation and always, without question, totally in charge. Then there was the compelling mystery about him, a secret so obvious that you could almost touch it.

In the few remaining seconds before Stormy fell asleep, she relaxed in the security of his aegis and didn't think about the mysterious meeting taking place back at the hotel.

CHAPTER THIRTEEN

STERLING AND I INTRODUCED OURSELVES TO the man who sent the note. He introduced himself as Karl Jones, and invited us to join him at his table in the corner of the lounge.

"Yes, I know of you, Mr. Barr, even though we have never met. Mr. Stanford, you are unknown to me. My request was only to speak with Mr. Barr, and the subject may not involve you. Therefore, I will allow Mr. Barr to determine if you should be party to our conversation."

"I have no objection to Mr. Stanford's participation in our meeting," I replied.

"Very good. Do either of you know a Mrs. Richter?" he asked without preamble.

Sterling and I both feigned ignorance, and I answered for both of us. "Who?"

"I believe you heard me correctly," he declared.

"I heard you correctly, but I still ask—who is she? Is she someone I should know? I assure you I do not. Better the question, why would you or anyone else ask me such a question?"

"I have my reasons," he stated.

"Did those reasons occasion you to travel here? Or are you just on vacation?" I facetiously asked.

"My reasons are my own," he stated curtly.

"No!" I retorted. "In choosing to come here and interrupt my life, you have made those reasons relevant to me and you shall disclose them."

"You can require me to do no such thing." He stood. "Our conversation here is through, I think."

"I think not," I said. "Sterling, would be you so kind as to inform the proper authorities that we have a gentleman here who is traveling with false papers?"

Sterling rose without speaking and departed the lounge.

"Who do you think you are, making such an accusation?" Karl almost shouted.

"I am the person with whom you are going to cooperate unless you want to spend the next few weeks arranging for proper papers and an exit visa."

"What evidence do you have that my papers are not correct?"

"Just a hunch. Are you willing to call my bet?"

We sat for a while in silence.

"First," he said, not giving any ground, "I must tell you that Mrs. Richter is in grave danger. If you know her or of her whereabouts, she must be warned."

"If I ever run across such a lady I'll pass your information along."

"So you won't admit you know her?"

"Let's not waste any more of our time; I'm sure Sterling

and his friends will be along shortly," I said. I leaned back and motioned to the waiter for drinks.

"All right, all right. I still believe you know her or could contact her if the need arose."

The waiter arrived and took our drink order.

"Go on," I nodded.

"I am taking a risk here because you may think me mad by the end of my narration."

"I doubt I will, but please continue," I said as our drinks arrived.

"I am in the employ of a private security firm; their identity as well as mine is unimportant, as you will come to learn. You need not look for us in the Yellow Pages. We are, shall I say, a product of the Iraq War.

"We have been retained, through intermediaries—by some person or entity or entities unknown to us—to protect Mrs. Richter."

"From what?" I asked.

"From being killed."

"Who wants to have her killed and for what reason?" I asked.

"That we don't know, believe me. It would make our job much easier if we knew."

"How, then, do you know her life is in danger?"

"We first operated on the belief that we wouldn't have been hired to protect someone if no threat existed."

"Reasonable," I muttered.

"More convincing, however, is the fact that at least two

and possibly three attempts have been made on her life since we were retained."

He then went on to describe the events Stormy had related to me.

It was my turn to sit quietly and digest his disclosures.

After a moment he said, "I warned you that you might think me mad. Unless, of course, Mrs. Richter has told you a similar story."

CHAPTER FOURTEEN

I ENTERED HER ROOM WITH THE STEWARD, who was bringing her a bed tray of tea and scones. She was waking and stretched like a cat just standing from a long nap.

"Good morning," I greeted her. "I hope you had a good night's sleep."

"Ross," she said, startled at my presence and pulling the sheet up. "I must look awful."

"No, you look great. Stormy, we're going to leave earlier than scheduled. I am sorry. I know that you and Linda had plans for today."

"I thought we couldn't leave—has the weather changed?"

"No. But our mode of transportation has."

I saw concern gather in her eyes and I reached out and brushed her cheek with the back of my fingers. "This is just a precaution," I soothed. "I will explain everything at breakfast."

I went down to the glass-enclosed breakfast veranda and was served coffee. I had never adjusted to having tea in the morning. The day was overcast, as promised, and *Sea Witch* would stay in anchorage another day.

Linda and Sterling arrived with Stormy, who took the chair I had pulled out for her.

"Good morning, Ms. Stormy," greeted Sterling.

"Cut out that Ms. Stormy thing, or I will start calling you 'Your Excellency,'" she threatened good-naturedly.

"Fair enough," he replied.

The steward finished serving breakfast and withdrew.

"This may take a minute," I said. I related to the girls my conversation with Karl.

"He knows everything you do and nothing relevant that you do not," I finished.

"So someone *is* trying to do me in," she concluded. "How bizarre … there are people trying to kill me and people trying to save me, and I don't know either of them."

"It appears to be true," I said.

"Does this Karl know I am here?"

"No," I assured her, "he is confident that I can contact you, however."

"Did he—did *they* kill the man that was trying to shoot me?"

"It would have been futile for me to ask. But as to the attempted mugging, I got the impression that there was only one attacker the night you walked home. The second man you saw running behind the villain was probably one of theirs; he must have prevented the attack on you and was probably the person who returned your purse.

"As to the car incident, it could have been either chance or the first attempt on your life. Either way, I got the idea that they had you under surveillance even then."

"We must find out who these people are," she said despondently.

"No- We must answer another question first."

"Really?"

I tried to think of a way to inform Stormy of what we knew without causing her more alarm, a way to depersonalize the seriousness of her situation.

"Permit me a little legalese to simplify and illustrate," I requested. She nodded.

"Let us say that the party of the first part is out to do you harm, and the party of the second part learned of the intentions of the party of the first part before their first attempt on your life. Furthermore, the party of the second part engaged the party of the third part to thwart the efforts of the party of the first part. Does that make sense?"

"No!"

"OK. Simply put someone wants you dead and someone else wants you alive."

"Oh. The party of the first part and the party of the second part?"

"Yes."

"Why didn't you just say so?"

"I thought I did."

"Seems unlikely."

"I agree. But, unlikely as it is, it is borne out by the facts." I paused. "The threshold question remains: Why are the parties of the first part and the second part so driven to achieve opposing results?

"Yea, so why?"

"I don't know but therein lies both the motive and the answer," I concluded. "Once we learn the motive behind their actions, we will be able to identify the parties."

"So, do we have a new plan?" Sterling asked.

"No—we have a new direction for our investigation. But we must stick to our original plan for now."

"What original plan?" Stormy asked.

"Plan A," I answered. "And Plan A requires that you and I depart as soon as you can be ready. There is no time to pack—your things will be taken to *Sea Witch*."

CHAPTER FIFTEEN

"SORRY FOR THE BUMPY RIDE," I SAID TO Stormy over the headset of the twin Beech King Air 200 as the two three-bladed turbo props screwed their way through the heavy air just above the ocean. We were two souls in an aircraft designed for eight and our short flight time allowed for a minimum fuel load. Even so, I held our speed to just above the stalling point to mitigate the beating we were taking from the same storms that delayed the departure of *Sea Witch*.

Stormy was securely belted into the co-pilot's seat next to me and was fixated on the wave tops, which rose less than fifty feet below us, and the overcast ceiling not more than one hundred feet above.

"We'll have a smoother ride once I climb above this, but I want to be sufficiently far from St. Cats first."

She sat, brooding.

"There is no cause for concern; we'll be at our destination in a few hours."

"I'm not concerned," she said finally. "I was just thinking about all my new things, left back on *Sea Witch*."

"Don't worry. Where you're going, your clothing needs will be minimal and met."

"Where I am going? Surely you're going, too. After all—you are flying the plane!"

"True, but I am leaving as soon as you deplane."

"Is this another one of your plans?" she asked inscrutably.

"No, it is still Plan A, which now includes an unscheduled departure from St. Cats and an equally unscheduled stopover at a small private cay nearby, named Amelia Cay. The area is home to a free clinic for island children, which is run by a lady doctor whose company I am sure you will enjoy."

"So. Once again, clothes-less, I am compelled to stay on a strange island while you go gallivanting around somewhere."

"Stop being so petulant and let me protect you," I said easily. "I had to find a place for you to hole up until we could re-board *Sea Witch*. It had to be somewhere with dockage capable of handling *Sea Witch* and an airstrip capable of handling this King Air. And it had to be someone who would take us on short notice."

"OK. So why can't you stay?"

"Trust me when I say it is prudent that I do not. Besides, I need to visit some old friends and beg their help in what could be Plan B."

After we landed and taxied back to the large complex that acted as a children's hospital, we were met by a woman in scrubs whose long, blond hair was tied up in a ponytail. As she approached the King Air, Stormy asked, "Is this the doctor you mentioned?'

"Yes."

"You didn't mention that she was also beautiful."

"Nope," I said as I extended the airstair and motioned for

Stormy to exit first. We stood next to the plane as Dr. Nel Benet strode up with a smile.

"Dr. Benet, I would like to introduce Mrs. Samantha Richter" I said.

"Call me Nel—short for Nellie, which is short for I won't tell what." The doctor grinned, holding out her hand. Stormy held out her own in a fast handshake.

"They call me Stormy."

"Not Sam?"

"No-- that was my husband's nickname." Stormy said quietly.

"Was?" Nel asked softly.

"My late husband."

Nel blinked. "Oh. I'm sorry for prying."

"No problem." Stormy tried a slight smile.

It was then that I decided to butt in. "I hate to interrupt, Nel, but I want to apologize ..."

"For dropping in on me this way?"

"And—"

"Bringing a guest?"

"And—"

"Just assuming it would be all right?"

"Uh, yeah. That too." I tried to look sheepish.

"Oh, hell babe, don't you think I am used to that by now? Don't answer."

Turning to Stormy, Nel said, "In truth I am delighted to have some adult female company for once. I understand you are in need of clothing?"

Stormy nodded. "I am embarrassed to say so, yes."

"Don't be embarrassed—with that clod you are lucky to have any clothes on at all." Nel snickered. "Would you be willing to help around the hospital with the kids while you're here?"

"Oh, I would love to." Stormy exclaimed.

"Well, then you are in luck. You look about the same size and shape as me and we have plenty of scrubs."

Nel and Stormy walked toward the hospital, already chatting like old friends. Before they entered, Nel turned and yelled at me, "Well, get on outta here, babe! Stormy and I can take care of ourselves." With a wink she turned and disappeared, with Stormy, into the dark interior of the clinic.

CHAPTER SIXTEEN

THIS WAS THE LARGEST GATHERING AT which he had ever been present. For matters of secrecy, very few members of this select group ever assembled at any one place or time; this would be the last such assembly.

Almost all communication was by fax machine and the faxes were destroyed as soon as possible after being read. Email was bullshit—a direct line to the Feds.

He mingled among his minions, offering encouragement and praise for their accomplishments to date.

He thought back to how he had first devised his plan and how easily he had implemented it. In the beginning, he'd recruited from random small meetings where bellicose far righties or far lefties would rant about almost identical and mostly imagined wrongs within the system. Each side felt left out of the "American Dream," and each had their own fix to the problem. The problem was that no one would listen or pay heed to them.

Here was fertile ground where he could grow a cadre of protagonists to carry out his personal agenda.

He was not the first to make such use of such discontent, this he had learned from history classes in the ivy-coated halls of his exclusive private schools. Marx had used the peasants of Russia, Hitler the unfortunates subjugated by the Treaty of Versailles, even Mark Antony, those untimely weaned from Nero's teat. And he had no such grandiose dreams as they.

Race, religion, and economic position have always been the great dividers of society. Race and religion are fixed, mostly circumstance of birth, and very little ever changes except the rhetoric. Economic well-being fluctuates and the pool of the discontent changes. Yet there is always a pool of discontent.

Even so, there is a critical threshold of discontent that must be crossed before the pool reaches critical mass and rises up to invoke historic change. The recent meltdown of the world economic system did not come near to crossing the threshold, but it swelled the ranks of discontent.

In any large group there are radicals ready to act in advance of the main body.

These individuals are the most vulnerable to suggestions of actions that they deem would serve their cause. Yet care had to be taken in choosing his team, because he was not looking for fanatics or martyrs. He wanted a cadre of personnel who believed they could make big changes with small acts.

His recruits were not trying to become leaders of a great revolution; they would be happy just to make surgical strikes at the foundation of the current system of greed, avarice, and corruption infecting the current economic system.

As he walked among them, he knew he had picked wisely. If this was a true or just cause, he would almost feel pride in what he had accomplished. These misfits and nitwits had coalesced into a cohesive group—they were sharp; they were ready. This last gathering was a pep rally for the core group. They, in turn, would bolster and invigorate the others.

They thought of themselves as modern minutemen, answering the call for justice and then melting away, back from whence they came with the conclusion of their duty. Each operated independently and on the basis of opportunity. No mission was to be carried out if any risk presented itself.

The fact that any mission could be aborted at will, along with their belief in the justness of their actions and that they would go unpunished for their deeds, enabled their desire to carry out the mission. They believed they would go unpunished because no motive could be discerned from their actions. No connection between them and their targets existed. Although a pattern would soon emerge, a pattern alone would not endanger their identities.

Even with all the precautions, the group needed a safety net.

The strange circumstances that led to the death of Samantha Richter's shooter could not be unraveled, nor had it been repeated. At least, nothing similar had been reported. Due to the independent actions of each member and the looseness of their connections, it was conceivable that other members had suffered similar fates. But it was unlikely that such an event would go unreported.

That had left only one item to cover. He set up a legal defense fund in an offshore account to pay for any members' attorney's fees in the event that any of them were apprehended. The bills would be submitted through an offshore post office box, reviewed by him, and, if approved, an equal sum of money would be sent to that member's designee to give the attorney.

The members were told that, prior to their firing a shot, there would be little risk of serious penal action—no license or registration is required to carry a long gun, and unless the gun has been recently fired, no charge of intent to harm would stand up in court. Up to the point of firing, the worst offense that could be filed against them would be a trespassing charge.

They were instructed to hire their own consul if the need arose and only if the need arose, because attorneys cannot divulge their clients' communications violating the law unless the violation has not yet occurred. But if an attorney is told by a client that the client intends to commit a criminal offence, the attorney is obligated to report this information to law enforcement.

Each member was advised to surrender and offer no resistance if challenged by law enforcement personnel. They were instructed to lawyer up and shut up.

They never suspected he was their reason for being. He always allowed others to promote and implement the agenda they thought their own.

He moved among them as a shadow. His true identity, as well as his physical features, was always disguised as was the true purpose of his plan.

The success of his operation lay with his ability to keep hidden his true purpose. His only purpose—his obsession. Revenge!

While his crew of recruits were creating murder and mayhem for what they believed to be the common good, they were actually punishing his enemies for the humiliations they visited on him and for his exile from the very ranks he was now determined to destroy. The only future communication necessary among the group would be provided by the news media. Each member could plan his actions or inaction based on what they learned from the daily press about the failures or successes of others. They could keep score by independently checking off the targets from *The List*.

He knew someday that some person or happenstance would expose the artificial purpose of this group. But nothing would lead to the real motive behind these crimes, or to him.

He sensed the meeting was coming to an end. He knew that they all understood that time was of the essence and that the season—the season of death and taxes—was about to close. He would drift away now, as the others also departed. He was someone who was always almost just remembered … but whom no one could put a finger on.

CHAPTER SEVENTEEN

SEA WITCH, UNDER THE COMMAND OF HER regular Captain, had made its way to Dr. Benet's island to pick up Ross and Stormy. Ross had arrived a mere few hours before *Sea Witch*'s arrival. Linda and Sterling had boarded earlier from a neighboring island where *Sea Witch* had made a stop to fully provision for an extended voyage, in the event that such a voyage became necessary.

While the foursome made their separate ways to the rendezvous at Dr. Benet's island, the newscasters blared the results and, by the end of the week, declared that nine separate attacks, resulting in the deaths of fifteen men, had occurred in the last week alone. None of the perpetrators were identified or detained.

Additionally, two abortive attempts were made in which no one was injured and no suspects found.

All had boarded, said their goodbyes to Dr. Benet, and were now safely at sea.

It was as obvious to me as to Stormy, Sterling, and Linda that dark forces were at work, and that the recent deaths went well beyond random acts of murder. These violent acts were being perpetrated by multiple supporters of some plot as yet unknown to all but themselves. There were some clues, however.

All of the victims were among the wealthiest people on earth. They were all American citizens, all killed on American soil. All were on *The List.*

Was this the nexus to Stormy—her wealth? There was one more interesting item: all were men.

Stormy was not mentioned in any of the stories. Possibly her one public near miss had been overlooked by the media.

"Have we come up with a total number of killed that fit the pattern we see developing?" I asked out loud.

Stormy, Linda, Sterling, and I were seated around the table in front of the television with an open line on a separate monitor to two of my researchers back in the States, who shared the split screen. They had worked for my law firm and continued to assist me when needed.

One of the two said, "Yes sir. To date, twenty-eight killed, none wounded, and five blotched attempts on three different persons."

"Explain," I requested.

"There were eight men killed before the attack on Mrs. Richter that fit the pattern," he said. "Six immediately after, and fifteen in the most recent round of attacks. There are five failed attempts, if you include the three made against Mrs. Richter. I need to qualify the twenty-eight figure, because one of the deceased—the bodyguard—was probably not an intended victim but mere collateral damage."

"I am sure his wife will appreciate the distinction," Linda grimly stated.

We all fell silent for a moment, realizing these numbers represented actual lives lost and other lives forever changed.

"Just the UHNWI's then," I interposed.

"The what?" asked the researcher.

The Ultra High Net Worth Individuals.

"Is that what they call them now?"

"That's it and thank you, gentlemen. Keep your noses to the CPUs and advise us of anything—and I mean anything you discover," I said, flipping off the monitor and breaking the connection.

"There is one other exception to the pattern regarding Stormy," Linda noted.

"What might that be?" I asked.

"Stormy is a female, if you haven't noticed."

"Good point. And I have noticed."

"Why does someone want to kill me, then?" asked Stormy.

"Give me until morning to figure that out," I replied. "Meanwhile, it's bedtime. Any more speculation is a waste of time and rest."

"What do you mean, a waste of time?" Stormy flared. "It's my life, you jerk!"

I thought about how my words had sounded from her end. "I stand sufficiently rebuked," I responded. "I apologize for acting so cavalier. In all of my years of practicing law, I never won a case by speculation—I believe in facts. I am sorry if I seem arrogant. It's a common malady among trial lawyers."

She nodded, seeming a little embarrassed by her hasty words. "I forgive you."

"I am doing my best to help you."

"I know. I just get worried."

"I know you do, and I should have considered your feelings." I placed my hand over hers, gently. "Shall I see you to your cabin?"

"If you wish."

CHAPTER EIGHTEEN

HE HAD SEEN THE SAME NEWSCASTS AS everyone else by now. The tally of the dead was rising, along with his satisfaction.

Even the unrest and fighting in the Middle East along with the usual political acrimony could not find space for a by-line in the midst of the current media frenzy.

The murder of America's wealthiest dominated the news.

At first he delighted in the coverage his revenge was generating, but he now craved the one act of revenge he desired most.

He would have preferred to suggest particular targets, but that would have raised suspicions about his motives and that could not be risked.

His creation had morphed into a thing in and of itself. No one, least of all himself, had any control over it. It had become open season on the mega-wealthy.

There was always the chance that it could not be contained. If even a few fanatics misinterpreted what was taking place, some might go about indiscriminately shooting anyone they deemed rich. That sort of undisciplined shooting spree would drive the true targets into hiding before they could be harvested.

He continually reminded his men that terminating one average billionaire was equal to killing one thousand average millionaires.

He had risked enough when he suggested a single target whose name was not on *The List*. Much discussion followed, but his suggestion was eventually taken. That murder would bring him closer than ever to getting revenge for the most humiliating event of his life.

Even so, he remained disappointed as he searched another day's news and nothing was mentioned about Mrs. Samantha Gail Richter.

CHAPTER NINETEEN

"YOU LOOK UNUSUALLY PENSIVE," STORMY pronounced as we sat alone in *Sea Witches*' cockpit, watching the helmsman steer us to nowhere in particular.

"Are we still on Plan A?" she prodded. "And what the hell is Plan A, anyway?"

"Sorry. I am, by coincidence, reviewing Plan A," I replied. "It's a good plan in that it is keeping you alive. But it is not solving your problem."

"What is Plan A supposed to accomplish?" she inquired.

"Keeping you alive."

"That's all?"

"That is not enough?"

"Well, of course. But it seems that you're the one who thinks that it's not good enough."

"I presumed that I would have a Plan B by now. I haven't found one yet because this whole affair lacks any discernable motive. All intentional acts require motive and opportunity. That is immutable. There is no shortage of opportunities for the perpetrators, yet no evident motive."

I paused.

"In your case, as in all cases, there must be a motive. We just haven't discovered it."

"And all I can do is sit here and take it?"

"Maybe Plan A has robbed the perps of opportunity," I continued, "thus inhibiting Plan B."

"How so?" Stormy frowned slightly.

"We are working so hard to hide you that the bad guy is unable to show himself."

"So, what do we do now?" she wondered aloud.

"We abandon Plan A and go to Plan B."

"Which is?"

"We give them the opportunity to kill you."

CHAPTER TWENTY

"CAN'T WE JUST USE SOMEBODY ELSE?"

"Who would you suggest?"

"Anybody! Well, not just anybody. Someone who is going to get shot anyway."

"And who might that be?"

"You know—what you said. One of those UHNM&M's.

"UHNWI's"

"Whatever! One of those American men on *The List* that haven't been killed yet. There must be over four-hundreds of them left."

"And that is why your idea is not tenable. We can't cover all of them and we don't know who will be targeted next."

"Maybe they have given up on me."

"I don't think so. They've already tried three times."

She sighed. "Why me?"

"You do seem to be an anomaly in this pattern. You've garnered special attention. The motive for your death may be additional to, or separate from, the motives of the other killings."

Stormy sat and listened with a resigned look on her face. "Damn. I hate Plan B," she muttered.

"Stormy, I will never allow any harm to come to you," I promised her solemnly. "Still, we must change our tactics if we are to truly protect you."

"By dangling the bait?" she asked sarcastically.

CHAPTER TWENTY-ONE

HE HARDLY NOTICED THE HEAD-LINES proclaiming the plight of his former colleagues, anymore. He now spent more time scanning the local sections of all the major newspapers for items printed in the society calendars that listed upcoming events for the social élite.

He remembered how, in the past, he was featured almost weekly. He had been one of them. No; he had been better than them. He was not born of them, nor had he arrived by way of a windfall. He'd toiled and sweated; he'd exploited each opening and every contingency to create opportunity where none existed.

They said he had drive and genius; he was exalted. That was before that bitch, before the investigation … .

There it was—an article about her giving a party for her employees. After having disappeared, she reappeared—just like a rabbit out of a hat.

Well, this time the rabbit would not get away.

CHAPTER TWENTY-TWO

NONE OF THEM KNEW WHO SENT THE FAX; none of them knew that their undisclosed handler had selected multiple operators for a single target. They would have been shocked to learn that *he* had all of their contact numbers. The others were limited to one or two other contacts, at the most.

In all, he had selected three. Their selection was due more to their proximity to the target and the further fact that none had been involved in a previous assignment. Each believed that they were the only person designated for this target. None of them knew that several attempts had already been made on her life and that none succeeded.

They might step on each other's toes, but they might not all follow through, either. He might not get another opportunity to finish her off and, in spite of his rancor for the entire group on *The List*, she was his prime target.

He knew that with the success of this mission he might lose some of his enthusiasm for the entire project. So be it. The bitch was worth all the others combined.

Nonetheless, the operation would go on—at least until the law change—and he would still enjoy the retribution to come.

CHAPTER TWENTY-THREE

STORMY STOOD BEHIND ME WITH HER HANDS on my shoulders as I sat reading through the invitation. She read along with me.

"So, am I just supposed to stand there and let them shoot me?"

"No," I reiterated for the n'th time.

"Am I going to at least get a bulletproof vest?"

"No. They would probably shoot you in the head, anyway."

"Ugh!"

"Stormy, we set up the opportunity—not they. We have control over the site. The opportunity is not real; it is only perceived to be real. This must work the first time, because we might not get a second chance."

"Why, because I will be dead?"

"No. Not that."

"You're sure! How can you be so sure?"

"Because you are not going to show up. At least, you're not going to show up when or where you are scheduled to."

"Won't they notice?"

"According to Plan B, not in time to find you."

CHAPTER TWENTY-FOUR

I MADE SURE THE VENUE WAS REAL—THE event, the invitations, the purpose … all were real. The guests were real, which caused us great concern. We couldn't allow them to be placed in any danger by our actions. To help accomplish the safety of the guests, the site of the party was impregnable, the number of guests limited to the barest minimum, and all were completely vetted.

No one on *The List* was considered. The party was restricted to only the hourly wage employees of one of the companies Stormy owned. The event was to be held at a hotel she owned. The party was to give recognition and bonuses to all of the staff of the company. No executive or management personnel were invited. None of the people attending would be on anybody's hit list, except for Mrs. Richter.

The much advertised appearance of Mrs. Richter was carefully planned. We controlled all access to the ballroom and only invitees would be allowed in. She would be vulnerable to a sniper from only three different locations. Each offered a possible shooter an escape route. Most importantly of all, each location could be observed and the escape routes blocked by my men, who would be well-hidden.

Stormy's route to the event was publicized in great detail and she was scheduled to arrive by limousine between 8 and 8:15 p.m. She was to stand outside the entrance at a reception table and greet her incoming guests. This would be the only time and place a would be assassin would have an opportunity to take a shot.

Of course, she would not be doing so. She would arrive at 7:30 p.m. in a non-descript, used sedan at a building adjoining the hotel. She would enter through the basement and then proceed to the ballroom.

The guests would arrive, beginning at 8:30 p.m. at the entrance to the hotel, as directed by the invitation, only to be told that Mrs. Richter was awaiting them in the ballroom.

This was the critical part of Plan B. The shooter, if any, would be in place no later than 7:45 p.m. to make sure that he did not miss her arrival, and he would be prepared to stay until around 8:30 p.m., in the event that she arrived late.

This would give us a window of approximately forty-five minutes to restrain the would-be assassin. In the event that one showed up.

For the job, Sterling and I gathered personnel from the ranks of specially trained friends and former associates—people Sterling and I had worked with before, people who owed me a few favors. Our call for help was promptly answered and we were humbled by the large response we received. More answered the call than we needed, so we only called on the ones least inconvenienced. We asked them to arrive in two days' time.

There were six, eight in all with Sterling and I. We met in the basement of the hotel where we had staged Stormy's employee party. The basement was restricted for all but hotel employees and they had all been given the night off and told not to return because the area was going to be fogged for pests.

The hotel was a perfect location for this plan for many reasons; none the least was its ease to provide accommodations for our group.

They were: John, a former CIA operative gone private; Doug, ex NYPD, retired; Abel, former FBI,SAC now operator of his own security firm; Charlie, currently on suspension from Detroit PD over a misunderstanding concerning a ruckus over an arrest; Billy, twenty year retired Seal and Mike-a very personal friend and confidant of long standing.

Sterling and I greeted each by name and exchanged brief updates on our immediate past lives in order to catch up since we had last talked to one another.

All had worn everyday casual clothing and would blend in with their surroundings.

"I am sorry we don't have time to reminisce as much as we would like, but we must get to business." I stated.

"Then let's get to it," said Mike, "I have a special interest in this matter."

"Yes, you and Sam ..."

"You remember."

"Yes, I ..."

Mike cut me off, "We'll have time to discuss it later, if I am correct, we need to move out."

"Right you are. We discussed the mission with each of

you before you arrived so you know its purpose. I need to split you all into three two man teams. Each team will man one of the designated three positions to be called Alpha, Bravo and Charlie positions.

"Yea, Abel."

"This is an opportunity that never occurs."

"What's that?"

"Our names."

"What about them?"

Why don't I be Alpha, Billy can be Bravo and Charlie can be Charlie."

Everybody laughed.

"Hay, why not?" Asked Charlie

"OK, so be it." said I

"We'll need leave now in order to arrive before 6 p.m., to give us a chance to take the assassin in his lair. Failing that, we could still close off his escape route." Said Mike

CHAPTER TWENTY-FIVE

"BASE TO ALPHA, BRAVO, CHARLIE, CHECK in," I spoke quietly into the headset. Each group leader signified that he was in position and operational. I acknowledged with a double click of my transmitter. Even though we had the best digital transceivers available, we had agreed that no names would be used in the presence of outsiders or on the air; there was no reason to risk any one's identity.

Each position checked in every fifteen minutes.

By 6:45 p.m., there was nothing.

7:00 p.m.—nothing.

7:15 p.m.—nothing.

7:20 p.m.

"Charlie position to base," the radio crackled. "I have a white male, medium build, carrying a small case that could hold a long gun if it was broken down."

"Roger that, hold your position and designate him Shooter One," I instructed. "We have plenty of time to see what develops. Don't check in again until he sets up."

"Roger."

7:30 p.m. Alpha, Bravo, nothing.

7:40 p.m.

"Alpha position to base. I have a Caucasian male, small build, also with a small case."

"Roger designate him Shooter Two, stand by and advise when he takes a position."

"Roger."

7:45 p.m. Nothing.

7:50 p.m.

"Charlie position to base, Shooter One has his weapon ready and appears operational."

Before I could reply, he continued in an excited voice. "Charlie position again, you won't believe this. I have eyes on another sniper that just moved into position behind my Shooter One."

"Has he joined your Shooter One, are they working together?"

"No! That is the strange thing about his location—he has no shot at the location we designated for our Client."

"Say again."

"There is no way he could take a shot at Stormy, even if she did arrive at her designated entrance."

"What's he doing?"

There was a pause. "He appears to have a silenced automatic hand gun with a laser sight, which he is playing on Shooter One's back."

"Does it look like he is going for a shot now?"

"Not at this time. He seems to be in no hurry."

"Designate him as UWM (unknown white male), and observe," I commanded.

"Roger."

"Alpha position, what is your man doing?"

"Just waiting."

"Bravo position, do you have any activity as yet?"

"Negative." No one has shown up as yet."

"You know, it looks like we have two would be assassins and for some strange reason an armed observer. Exactly why or what he is observing is a mystery." I mused.

"Well let's find out. Bravo team. Since no one has shown up at your location I want you to leave your position and assist Charlie position by very quietly disarming the UWM. Do not move him to the basement until we have secured both Shooter One and Shooter Two."

"Roger."

"Did you get that, Charlie and Alpha?"

"Affirmative," each replied.

"As soon as Bravo has secured the UWM you all take out Shooter One and Shooter two and we'll meet back at the barn"

"Roger," they said in turn.

"Sterling, would you please take over here until everybody gets back? I want to run upstairs and check on Stormy."

A nod.

"Have someone come get me when the group arrives."

I was standing near the door to the ballroom when Mike came in and touched my elbow to get my attention.

"How'd it go?" I asked.

"Pretty easy, both shooters one and two are definitely amateurs. The UWM is obviously a professional, but gave no resistance. How's the party going?"

"Great, Stormy is clueless to the events taking place outside—and happy because of it."

We returned downstairs to be met by three unwilling participants sitting handcuffed in hardback wooden chairs, facing a desk to which I walked and perched.

"Don't I know you?" one of them asked me.

CHAPTER TWENTY-SIX

I POINTED TO THE MAN WHO HAD ASKED THE question and looked at the Charlie Team leader. "Is this the UWM?"

He nodded.

I moved my gaze to Billy, the Bravo Team leader. He nodded in agreement.

"Take him to office 3-B, down the hall to your left," I said to Abel the Alpha Team leader. "Remove his handcuffs and get him something to drink, water or a cola. Lock him in and have someone stand guard outside the door."

Abel nodded and the UWM was removed from the room.

"I will talk to you later, Karl," I said as they left the room.

The door closed and I returned my attention to Shooter One.

"What is your name? I inquired in a civil tone.

Instead of answering my question, he began a rant.

"I am not going to tell you my name or anything else. You haven't read me my rights; you haven't given me my phone call. I want my lawyer. You can't arrest me; I haven't done anything."

"Are you going to cooperate?" I asked.

Silence.

I motioned Billy over and leaned near to him. In a stage whisper that couldn't be missed by the other perp, I said, "Get rid of him."

Billy and his team member moved and in an instant had Shooter One by his arms, lifting him out of the chair and hustled him out the door and down the hall.

Before the door had fully closed, a loud pistol shot rang out, followed by the sickening thud of a body falling to the floor.

The other perp, designated Shooter Two, slumped down in his chair, unconscious, held up only by his handcuffs. He soiled himself.

A chuckle ran through the men and they relaxed, knowing that their part of the job was over.

"Go home, go back to your lives," I said to them, trying to relax myself. "Once again, many thanks for being here when I needed you. Each of you know that I will always be around if you need me."

We exchanged handshakes and *abrazos* and they left the way they had come, unnoticed via the loading dock.

The perp we designated as Shooter Two was slowly coming to. I took off his handcuffs and grabbed him under his armpits from behind and lifted him off the chair. I pushed him toward the office across the hall from where we stood.

As we crossed the hallway, he halted our progress long enough to look to the left, in the direction the other shooter had been taken.

There was blood splattered on the wall and floor and a trail of blood leading down the center of the hallway, continuing to the bloody hair of Shooter One, who was being dragged by his heels to the exit at the end of the hall. His hair slopped blood along the floor like a mop as he was dragged along.

I tightened my grip on him in case he passed out again, but he threw up instead. I steered us both around his mess and shoved him into the doorway of a room designated 2-B. I closed the door behind me and proceeded to 3-B.

CHAPTER TWENTY-SEVEN

AS I MADE MY WAY TOWARD 3-B, I REMEMBERED my first meeting with Mr. Jones on St Cats. I knew then circumstances would cause our paths to cross again; just not so soon or under such conditions.

I decided it was time to bring him on board, if possible, and end this game of cat and mouse. I arrived at 3-B and asked Jack, the guard, where Mike, his team leader, had gone. As he opened the door for me to enter, he said, "Mike wanted me to tell you he had to get ready for a flight out of the country, and that he will see you soon." I nodded.

Karl Jones, or whatever name he was using now, sat in a chair in front of a desk near a large glass window that looked out onto the hallway.

He would not have been able to miss Shooter One being dragged down the hall.

"Pretty good act you guys staged," he said knowingly.

"I didn't think you would be fooled," I said appreciatively. "Anyway, it was not staged for your benefit."

"Was he hurt? It sounded like a hell of a fall."

"No. The plan was simply to trip him. Then they drugged him and added the fake blood and gore before they played the final scene for his co-conspirator. He will be all right in about half an hour."

"I imagine that your ruse will have its desired effect on the other perp and loosen his tongue," surmised Karl.

"I imagine it will," I said with a smile.

"So, what shall we do, you and I?" he asked.

CHAPTER TWENTY-EIGHT

"UNPLANNED AS IT IS, THIS MAY BECOME A fortuitous meeting for the both of us," I said as I took a chair across from him.

"How so?" he asked.

"Karl, shall I continue to address you as Karl?"

"For now."

"Alright, I need your total cooperation in order to execute the plan I have in mind."

"What about your cooperation?" he replied.

"I think you'll find my cooperation totally adequate; you will get the better of the deal."

"In that event, please go on," he said.

"First I need to know with whom I am bargaining."

"I already told you the truth back on St. Cats. We don't know the identity of our *de facto* employer."

"I believe you; I am more interested in you and your organization. Our little act notwithstanding, we do not kill people and I will not be in league with anyone who does; unless absolutely necessary, of course."

"Understood," he said, "but if we are to be honest with each other don't try to play naïve with me."

"How so?" I asked.

"I know more about you than you might think; for instance, I know what you did between college and the start of your career."

"Maybe, but not all."

"Enough to know these were some of the men or should I say, comrades in arms that you worked with during that time."

"Notwithstanding what you may or may not know, I want to know whether your men killed either of the two men that previously attacked Mrs. Richter."

"That's more than a simple yes or no answer," he hesitated.

"I need more than a simple yes or no answer," I replied.

He sighed. "You have time?"

"I have time."

"We were contacted and hired through intermediaries. That I've already told you, what I didn't tell you was our unknown employer not only wanted Mrs. Richter protected, he also required us to hire two private investigators that were presented to us, *fait accompli*. We were given no information about either of them, other than the bare necessities.

"At first we refused the job and to hire their men, but later relented. We needed the money and the extra help.

"We put Tom and John, as they were identified, on the payroll and had their papers authenticated by the State Board of Private Investigators. To our surprise, they passed. I still believe their papers are no more legit than the ones I used to enter St. Cats—the ones you used to call my bluff."

I couldn't help but indulge in a small smirk of satisfaction.

"They took right to the job, as if it were custom made for

them." he continued. "But their reports were sloppy and the hours they turned in overstated. We brought it up with our employer and were instructed to overlook their shortcomings, which we did."

"Did you get many instructions from your employer?"

"When we refer to communication with our employer, you know we are going through a third party," Karl reminded me. "We didn't receive instructions very often, and only in the beginning." He paused. "One unusual item—they implied that Tom and John would only be needed for a short time."

"Were any dates mentioned?"

"No."

I nodded thoughtfully. "I gather that Tom and John reported to you about the car incident, the mugger, and the shooter?"

"Yes, they reported that the car event was just chance and they reported the mugger was chased away unharmed."

"What about the shooter with the broken neck?"

"They disavowed any participation in his demise. Without any evidence or witnesses to the contrary, we could do nothing but believe them. We conveyed our concerns to our employer and advised that we could no longer keep them on our payroll. Before we got a response, Tom and John called in and quit."

"Didn't that end your employment?"

"No. When we did get a response, we were directed to continue with our commitment to protect Mrs. Richter and to use our own personnel. This occurred around the time I met you on St. Cats," he stated. "It was from our employer that we learned of you and of your whereabouts."

"Both times?"

"No. Just on Elizabeth Isle, where you and Mrs. Richter ducked out on *Sea Witch* before Tom and John could find either of you. I located you on my own at St. Catherine. That was after Tom and John quit our employ."

"Are you still working for your unknown employer?"

"That's why I am here today."

We both sat in silence for a while.

"Your turn," Karl said, "Why are you involved in whatever this is?"

"Me, I'm just a sucker for a damsel in distress."

"Yeah, we pretty much assumed," he said, his expression friendly. "What about the plan you mentioned?"

"I think you will like Plan C." I grinned.

CHAPTER TWENTY-NINE

STORMY AND I SAT IN THE LIVING ROOM OF the penthouse suite atop the hotel that had been host to all the activity earlier.

"So explain to me what Plan C is about," she demanded. "I still like Plan A the best."

"Understand that Plan C is not the end of it all—it is a path to the end."

"You mean I will have to suffer through a Plan D?"

"Probably."

"Do you know what Plan D is yet?"

"No."

"Great." She rolled her eyes. "Just tell me about Plan C, then."

"I made a deal with our new good friend Karl Jones and his organization to continue their commitment to protect you, but to do nothing."

"Why nothing?" she asked.

"Because I am protecting you, and too many chefs spoil the soup."

"OK."

"Also, we gave them both of the men that were out to kill you today."

"What are they going to do with them?"

"Turn them over to the police and get credit for catching them. That will bolster their reputation among their clients, especially your unknown protector. It may get them more clients—and I certainly don't need the recognition."

"I bet the business of protecting people is good in light of recent events," she said.

"No doubt. However, our benefit from the bargain is that me and my little troop of do-gooders will remain anonymous and be able to pursue your problem unheralded."

"I've been meaning to ask about your little troop of do-gooders; I didn't get to meet any of them."

"How about this, you don't ask and I won't tell?"

"If you're going to be like that, then at least tell me about the guys who tried to kill me?" She said irritatedly. "Won't they blab about your little charade?"

"I think they have made their minds up not to say anything. Even if they did, no one would believe such a fantastic story." She and I locked gazes; I moved over and sat next to her on the couch.

"Did you learn anything from them about why they tried to kill me?" she asked, her gaze downcast.

"I learned volumes. After the little drama we produced by 'getting rid of' the first shooter, the second one would not shut up. He said they had joined a group of zealots that were out to change the economic system of the U.S. To summarize his long dissertation on the state of the union and how they are going to save it, I will just tell you that they are a bunch of nuts killing rich people off a list supplied to them by an unknown person or persons. He never heard of you before his attempt to kill you. He was furnished your name, a picture of you, and where you would be so he could kill you. He had no idea there was another shooter, and likewise for the other one. This thing is like a hydra—you cut off one head and another pops up. I gathered the details of their operation and finally decided that he didn't possess any worthwhile intel to aid us in our pursuit to solve your dilemma. I left his further interrogation up to the others that would follow me."

She grasped my hand, moving it to her lap and clutching it there tightly. Her gaze fixed on mine, urging me to reveal something helpful or good.

"I did ask him if he knew whether there was a deadline of any kind, and he admitted that 'the season would soon be over.' I asked when, and he said he didn't know, but he would be told when it was over. I asked what the season was and who would tell him, and he said he didn't know."

"Did you believe him?" she asked.

"I believe what he told me was true." I paused.

"You have doubts," she declared.

"I doubt he told me everything. He was holding something back, but I could not design a way to bring it out."

"So this whole exercise failed to yield any useful information about my particular situation."

"Except that Karl and his group will be acting in our interest in the future, and they will attempt to obtain the identity of their mysterious client. That information may be the only way we can learn the motive."

"That will be a conflict of interest for them, will it not?"

"It will, but they don't care. They feel betrayed by their employer because of the two people they had to hire. If Tom and John murdered your attacker while on their payroll, Karl and his associate would lose their license, at the bare minimum."

She sighed. "So we still don't know who is trying to kill me."

CHAPTER THIRTY

IT DIDN'T MAKE THE FRONT PAGES OF MOST papers and was not a lead item for the talking heads. A story about a couple of men with guns caught casing a hotel was not the stuff of a lead story. Some labeled them terrorists; neither had a prior record of misconduct or fanatic group membership, and, most importantly, they weren't talking.

Apparently, none of the reporters had made a connection with Stormy, the bitch, and probably never would.

Why were there only two gunmen? Did one get away, or did only two show up? Probably the latter. No surprise there—that was the reason he had selected three.

Christ, he thought. *That was the last time I could use these men for an attempt on Stormy's life.* There had been three attempts on her life, involving four attackers, and all had failed. Four attempts and five attackers, if you included the time he had tried to run her over on Rodeo Drive. Shit, how could she be so lucky?

All this damn work and preparation had been for nothing!

Actually, not entirely for nothing. He was still making deep cuts into the core of the society he hated almost as much as he hated Stormy.

There was no other option left to him. He would do what he should have done from the start—he would have to kill her himself. It was much riskier. But the satisfaction of watching her die would be worth the extra risk.

CHAPTER THIRTY-ONE

THE NEXT DAY, STORMY AND I SOARED OVER the southwestern United States and Mexico on our way back to *Sea Witch*, which was awaiting our arrival in the Windward Islands. We were comfortably ensconced aboard her Hawker-4000, cruising forty-three thousand feet above those who would do her harm.

"We must go back over every aspect of your life. You are the only person who has had multiple attempts on your life—it seems that, for some reason, you are a priority in this killing spree. There must be someone in your past who has a terrible grievance against you. To put it more succinctly, know it or not, you have seriously pissed somebody off."

"In spades!" came a deep voice from the door to the flight deck. "Am I interrupting anything?" the voice asked.

"Captain!" Stormy said. "Not at all—we've been waiting for you."

"We have?" I chuckled. "This is the second time in two days I have had the pleasure and surprise of seeing you, Mike," I called. "What's it been, over four years since we were in Portugal together?"

"The second time in two days?" Stormy asked, puzzled.

"I guess I forgot to tell you, Stormy," Mike stated casually. "I was one of the team members with Ross yesterday."

"And you and your men did a damn good job of clearing Mr. Karl Jones out of the way. As a result, the other teams were able to subdue the two shooters without incident," I said. "Your business partner has a lot of talents unknown to you."

"I guess you two forgot to tell me a lot of things," Stormy joked. "I knew that you and Captain Butler were friends—I just didn't realize the depth of your friendship."

"We have a habit of coming to each other's aid, when needed," I explained. "It is *you* that have been holding out on me," I accused her jovially. "Is Mike one of the mutual friends you mentioned on our first meeting; the one who insisted I was your only hope?"

"I guess I'll have to own up to that, Ross," Mike admitted. "After all, everyone knows that you are—"

I cut him off, "—a sucker for a damsel in distress!"

"What have you been doing, anyway? Still trying to ignore the rest of the world?" Mike asked.

"Trying without success, apparently," I answered. "What about you?"

Stormy answered for him, "You know that he and my late husband started our air charter business together? Mike was Sam's personal pilot and confidant even before we were married. He has remained mine, also."

"You're the CEO of the air charter business, right?" I asked.

"Yes," he replied. "I took over after Sam died."

"Not only that, but he is the second largest shareholder," Stormy added.

"Mike, if you are the high and mighty CEO of this outfit, what are you doing driving the plane?"

"Same as you, I reckon; I love flying." He grinned.

"I don't blame you. I sure wouldn't mind getting my hands on this bird," I said.

"I heard you did a pretty fancy job of deck hopping while trying to scare the wits out of Stormy in a King Air."

"She told you?" I gave her a mock glare.

"Said you were pretty good, too," Mike flashed a grin.

"Beats sitting in the back," I replied lazily.

"Look," Mike said, "I was in on the interrogation of the perps after you left. If Stormy has any other questions about what we learned, I can answer them. If you'd like, you can go up front and take the left seat."

"Deal!"

CHAPTER THIRTY-TWO

"ARE YOU GOING TO TELL ME?" STORMY asked Mike after Ross had closed the cockpit door behind himself.

"Tell you what, Stormy?"

"You know."

"Stormy, it is not my place to add to anything Ross has told you. If Ross wants you to know more or if he thinks you need more information, I'm confident he will disclose it to you."

"Mike, I already know a lot. I just can't fathom why he dropped out! And when I first met him he made it clear, in no uncertain terms, that he did *not* want to discuss it with me."

"No one, not even he, can ever know all the reasons. But he did mention once that he was tired of suffering fools."

"You knew him before he changed his name and went into self-imposed exile, didn't you?" Stormy asked.

"We knew each other, and Sam, too, long before you met Sam," Mike admitted. "Back when we were young and daring."

"I wish he would stop trying to lead a double life," said Stormy

"He is not leading a double life—he is leading a second

life. The first one is over. You have heard people say that they wished they could live their lives over again, knowing what they do now? Well, he is getting to do it."

"What about his ex-wife and his kids?"

"She has a very rewarding life of her own choosing and the kids have grown up. I visit them occasionally. They have lives of their own and are quite happy."

"That's it?" Stormy said, disappointment written all over her face.

"Well there is more to it than that, but there were no tragic circumstances, no deaths, terminal illnesses or warrants out for their arrest, if that's what you mean," Mike said smiling.

"No, that's not what I meant, it's just that I cannot understand."

"You could say they had an epiphany."

"You mean a visit by a deity?" She asked louder than intended.

"No, not an Epiphany, an epiphany, a perception, a deep insight."

Seeing that Stormy was listening but not understanding, he went on. "They had the realization that they could become the embodiment of their dreams, in their current lives, for real, not just virtually; they could become their *alter egos*."

"Their what?" she shouted.

*"The persons that only their dreams would allow," he answered. "You see; t*hey could become the people they had been denied to be by their successes."

"Their successes?" asked Stormy." I know about Ross, nothing about his wife."

"His wife was a pediatric neurosurgeon, and quite accomplished."

"Oh." Stormy seemed impressed.

"Success comes at a high price," Mike continued. "There is forced conformity, playing by the rules, loss of privacy, and the entire time acting like you enjoy it. They discussed the issue with their kids, and the children were very supportive. They arranged for a quiet divorce and slipped away to begin the rest of their lives on their own terms."

"Didn't they love each other?"

"Definitely, but it became lost in the hassle of everyday life."

Dismayed Stormy asked, "What did they want to be?"

"Only they know for sure, but apparently Ross wanted to become just what he is."

"And his wife?"

"She just wanted to be able to help children on her own terms. To provide medical care. especially to those that would otherwise not get it."

"You don't mean ...?"

"Yes, Dr. Benet, but don't let Ross know I told you, he thought you would figure it out on your own, given time."

Stormy sat silent for a moment and then said, "I think I understand. More often than we'd like to admit, we all suffer from being trapped by our lifestyle... at least they had the courage to do something about it."

"Hmm," Mike grunted softly. "Not to change the subject, but your nephews contacted me several weeks ago. They sold their Lear Jet 60 and want to buy time on some of the aircraft in our fleet. They asked if we could let them have a preferred rate."

"Are you sure?" Stormy frowned. "I spoke with them just last week and they didn't mention anything to me ..."

Mike nodded. "They may have made some overleveraged hedges and can't pick up their shorts."

"Do you think they are really hurting?" asked Stormy.

"It is very probable. They inherited their father's money, but not his business acumen," said Mike.

"They had all the money they could ever need or spend," remarked Stormy. "What happened?"

"The usual—the inherited rich can usually live for generations on their ancestors' wealth, and most do. There are some who think they can improve their lot, and most of them do not. Ergo: The way to make a small fortune is to start with a big one."

"Are the nephews a lost cause?" Stormy asked.

"Unless some miracle happens ... they probably have about four months before the final call is made on their shorts."

CHAPTER THIRTY-THREE

THE EMTS HAD BEEN TOLD WHEN THEY WERE dispatched that this was a shooting victim and, according to the dispatcher, was some sort of a big shot; the pun obviously intended. They rushed their patient through the double doors of the ER into the trauma center, where a trauma team was waiting. The EMTs hung around as the trauma team went through their drill, even though their collective experience dictated this victim was beyond their skills.

A gunshot victim was nothing unusual around this place, but this time the Chief of Staff was present.

Noting the unusual presence of the Chief of Staff one of the EMT's said to the other, "Apparently the dispatcher was right about the victim being somebody."

The on-call ER doctor was able to maintain the patient's vitals by use of the life support system. Using life support was SOP in situations like this. Hopefully it gave the ER team time to evaluate the patient's condition. It could not prevent the inevitable and its efficacy was measured in hours. Sometimes they induced a coma; even hypothermia, but in this case---the EMG revealed that substantial irreversible brain damage had occurred.

The doctor turned to the Chief of Staff. "I'm sorry; I know he is a friend of yours. But there's little I can do. I doubt he'll last through the night. I'll have him moved from life support and his vitals will flat line within an hour or so and I can `pronounce` him."

"Don't do that I want to transport him," said the Chief of Staff.

"Good lord, why?" asked the doctor. "There is nothing to be gained by it."

"Not necessarily," replied the Chief of Staff. "For one thing, he will leave your shift alive. Think of all the paperwork that will save you."

"Roger that," said the former army doctor. "I'll sign him out this minute."

"Oh, and I will need all his records, as well," declared the Chief of Staff.

"You sign for 'em and you got 'em," said the doctor, who left to sign the release. Two tours of duty in Iraq had taught him not to buck the brass.

CHAPTER THIRTY-FOUR

THE AIRPLANE LANDED AT THE PRIVATE airstrip located high in the Alps. The G-3 had been configured as an air ambulance, but even with the reduction in gross weight and its few occupants, it used up all of the available runway before it groaned to a stop.

It was a clear night with a near full moon. As the plane taxied back down the ramp to a large hangar, the only facility on the strip, two immigration officers walked out of the hangar office. They crossed the tarmac to where the G-3 stopped.

They had been summoned earlier for the sole purpose of clearing one person through immigration. They didn't mind; they got extra pay and a perfectly legal tip for providing this service.

A large cargo door on the starboard side of the fuselage behind the wing opened hydraulically and began to lower. A gurney surrounded by a life-support apparatus and two technicians were lowered with it.

An ambulance pulled up next to the men and waited.

One of the immigration officers stepped forward and accepted some papers from the technicians. He was careful to check the name against a list on a hand held device for persons wanted for various reasons or prohibited to enter the country.

Not finding any matches and finding all the necessary paperwork in order, the officer stamped the passport and passed it along to one of the waiting ambulance drivers.

The gurney, its occupant, and the life support equipment were loaded into the ambulance. The cargo door retracted carrying the two technicians up with it and seamlessly folded into the airplane. The immigration officers watched as the graceful white airplane sped down the runway, gleaming between the runway lights, and shot almost straight up into the clear night sky. As if on cue, the runway lights blinked out.

On the flight deck the First Officer said to the Captain, "This is the second time I have had trouble getting the nose gear indicator to display up and locked."

"Log it and we will get it checked before our next flight," replied the Captain.

At the same time, the ambulance sped up the mountain toward the clinic.

As the officers returned to their vehicle, one remarked, "That is the fourth one this week, isn't it?"

"Without a doubt. And the second time I've missed supper. That brings the total to … what, twenty-two?" replied the other.

"I wonder what goes on up there. Someone spent a fortune fixing up that old asylum," said the first.

"I don't care," replied the other. "As long as we get the extra money and, of course, their papers are in order."

The first officer nodded. "Have you noticed that those poor souls never speak? They must be terribly ill."

"So they must. I have seen livelier looking gentlemen in coffins."

CHAPTER THIRTY-FIVE

"THE MORE WE LEARN, THE LESS WE KNOW," I surmised. We were back on *Sea Witch* and seated at the table in the main salon. Linda, Sterling, and I had already finished breakfast. Stormy was being served.

"Well, what *do* we actually know?" Linda questioned.

"I know one thing," Stormy said as she lifted a muffin from her plate. "Someone is trying to kill me."

"You and many others, it appears," agreed Sterling.

"Multiple victims attacked by multiple assassins. The assassins are all loosely connected zealots in pursuit of some common goal that appears to be governed by a deadline. It has been likened to a season of some sort, and appears to have an arbitrary ending," I added.

"The victims are of all ages and races and are all male," offered Linda.

"I am not a male!" piped up Stormy.

"And all are on *The List*," said Sterling.

"I am not on *The List*!" yelled Stormy.

"You are not on *The List*?" I asked, astonished.

"I am not on *The List*!" she repeated.

Sterling, Linda, and I looked at her in astonishment.

"I am almost on *The List*," she explained. "Sam was on *The List*. But after his death, the estate went through probate and applicable federal and state taxes were paid. These accounted to about one half of his estate. So that knocked me off *The List*.

"I still have more money than God; you might notice that God is not on *The List*, either," she joked.

"Then there has to be a direct connection between you and whoever is behind these attacks. Something in your past; you must think!" I urged again.

She shrugged, looking thoughtful.

"You mentioned that there was once a relationship that ended because of intervening circumstances," I prodded.

"Yes."

"Tell me about that, please."

"It was Lars Conrad. He was a self-made millionaire, and at a very young age.

"I never liked him. I actually disliked him—under all the polish he was crude and base. However, he assumed that I was to be his and he would have it no other way."

Agitation began to show in her features. "I refused him again and again. First I refused his advances, then his proposals, and yet he persisted over and over. He always ignored my refusals," she said.

"One evening I was attending a large gala given to honor his birthday. For the occasion, I had consented to go as his date. When the orchestra was on break, he took me up on the stage, picked up the microphone used by the bandleader, and called everybody to attention. He said he wanted to make an announcement.

"Without any knowledge on my part, he proposed marriage to me and forcibly grabbed me and kissed me hard in front of all the guests. I was shocked and repulsed by his behavior, and I backed away.

"I did not want to be involved in a scene with him in front of his friends and mine. I pretended embarrassment at all the eyes on us, and tried to simply walk away. But he took me by the arm, held me there, and demanded an answer. I tried to ease away again and he squeezed my arm harder. Seeing no other option available, I finally said 'NO! NO! I won't marry you. Now let me go!' Instead of releasing me, he glared at me and squeezed even harder.

"I slapped him hard across his face, and he finally let go. I ran off the stage and out the front door, hailed a taxi, and went home.

"I expected more trouble from him, but he was indicted for fraud the very next week. I never saw him again.

"So, as I said before—other circumstances intervened to my advantage, and I have not seen him since."

"Did you learn what became of him?" I inquired.

"I'm not sure," she answered. "I heard he lost everything and that he got probation and no jail time. He was ostracized by all of his friends and associates, however. They treated him like the plague."

"Is it possible that he still holds a grudge against you; could he be crazy enough to want to kill you for your treatment of him?" I asked.

"He could----It was many years ago, and we were both very young, but he was a man of singular purpose. Like the old saying, once he got a bone between his teeth, he wouldn't let go."

She sat quietly for a moment, then said reflectively, "I have known and heard stories of people who have lost great wealth. They cope badly."

"How so?" I asked.

"Their lifestyle change is so severe. It's not like they just lose their job, something ordinary people cope with all of the time. Money is like a narcotic; they can't live without it."

"Do they ever cope?" I asked.

"Many don't. Some resort to suicide, sometimes clothed as an accident or heart attack. A lot more turn to booze and drugs. Quite a few become born again or evangelical Christians and they seem to cope by renouncing all worldly goods."

"Does any of this bear on Lars?"

"Only in one way," she answered. "Even though you don't often mix with the fallen, you always hear about their circumstances."

"That seems odd ..."

"Not really. You see, they make a great topic for gossip and serve as a subliminal warning of 'but for the grace of God... .'"

"So?"

"And so, Lars did not kill himself, booze up, or get "born again"; he just vanished. Out of sight, out of mind. That's the reason I passed over him so briefly when you first questioned me about my relationships."

I could feel the effect of the ground swell through *Sea Witch*'s hull, which signaled that we were approaching the outer islands and nearing St. Catherine.

"Speaking of going, let's go to bed," I said.

"Really!" she exclaimed. "You feeling lucky?"

"I don't know—am I?"

"Not tonight, big boy."

"Just as well, we …"

"Just as well?"

"Well, not just as well."

"I should hope not." She stood with her hand pressed against her hips, elbows out, glaring at me.

I lowered my head and looked at my feet like a school boy caught trying to peak into the girls' locker room. How could any woman have this effect on me? "Of course. I meant only that we will be docking at St. George Harbor before dawn and on my watch; I'll need a cat nap and a clear head before entering the harbor."

"Will I be in danger back on St. Cats? The last time we just snuck in and snuck out …"

I had supplemented Plan C by arranging for Karl to come to St. Cats and keep a discrete eye on her for the next few days, although I didn't want to alarm her by telling her so. With such a good guard on her, she shouldn't need to worry about guarding herself.

"Possibly. But I don't foresee any great risk. I wouldn't take you there if I thought you'd be in great danger."

CHAPTER THIRTY-SIX

HE WATCHED THEM DOCK. THE ONLY ACTIVITY that had occurred since they docked was when several of the crew went ashore.

He knew she was there—the loose lips around the harbor had confirmed his suspicions.

He would kill her later today. He had not been able to smuggle any weapons onto the island, but that didn't matter. This would be up close and personal. Just the way he wanted it.

Once she came ashore, he would only need to wait for an opportunity to take her by surprise.

CHAPTER THIRTY-SEVEN

"AREN'T YOU GOING TO TELL US WHY ALL those murders occurred?" asked Linda.

"What makes you think I know?" I replied.

"Because I know you, and you're holding something back," Linda said.

"OK, you're right. I have a clue, but I want to verify a few facts first," I said.

"Do you know what this means?" I asked Stormy.

"That I'm no longer a target?"

I laughed kindly. "No, I am afraid that you still are. It means that there may be other means at work than what seemed to be obvious. However, no attacks have occurred off of U.S. soil—the only persons to approach you outside of the U.S. were there to protect you."

"Why were there no attacks outside the U.S.?" quizzed Linda.

"It probably has to do with the difficulty of transporting weapons now-a-days," Sterling offered.

"And?" asked Stormy.

"And so you and Linda can go ashore. I don't expect any

harm to come to you this trip, and you have yet to see St. George. Go shopping, have fun—you should be perfectly safe."

As I watched her leave to prepare for the trip, I decided that I had made the right decision in not telling her that Karl was going to be tailing them to keep her safe. Nor did I confide in her about Linda also knowing about Karl.

She needed some time to enjoy herself without being under the constant stress of fearing for her life.

CHAPTER THIRTY-EIGHT

I WALKED BACK TO MY OFFICE TO DO SOME research before disclosing my hypothesis about the motive behind the unexplained killing of mega-rich U.S. citizens.

I sat at my desk and accessed the legal research databases to which I continued to subscribe. These were not readily available to the public, but for use by attorneys only. But even without the sophistication of my sources, I could easily have confirmed my suspicions.

There it was, pending legislation in both Republican Led Houses of Congress to repeal the *Death Tax*. This was not unprecedented. A similar proposal had passed and been enacted into law.

It was the Economic Growth and Tax Relief Reconciliation Act of 2001 (EGTRRA). One of the Bush administration's first acts. The first installment to the "haves and have mores," the proposed tax policy had quickly been passed by the Republican-dominated House and Senate and was signed into law by the President. By 2003, it began decreasing the top rate on estate taxes and eventually repealed all estate taxes, making the rate 0%.

It was short lived, however, because a subsequently elected

Democratic Congress along with a Democratic President side-tracked the legislation soon after it took effect.

As it was only a few lucky heirs reaped benefits before EGTRRA was scrapped, but those few were able to save billions of dollars.

Now, however, it seemed certain that a new version of the former law would be passed. It provided for a complete repeal of all *Death Taxes* as of its' effective date.

A date expected to be within a few months, at most.

No right minded UHNWI would be caught dead before its enactment.

CHAPTER THIRTY-NINE

"ST. GEORGE IS AN EASY-GOING CITY FOR A modern port. It has the expediency necessary for commerce, mediated by the carefree attitude of island life," Linda said, "Look at the style of the architecture. It's a blend of tropical and English influences. The commercial and port districts are primarily occupied by brick buildings with common walls and the residential areas have wide streets. The dwellings are separated by lush lawns."

As they walked along, Stormy said, "There seems to be few tourists about for such a lovely city."

"St. Catherine is not touted by its inhabitants as a tourist destination. Our economy is based in banking and ships' registry, and we prefer it that way," answered Linda. "My lovely husband has played a great part in negotiating favorable treaties and trade agreements with our island neighbors and especially with most of Europe, Asia, and the Middle East. In addition, our stable democratic government draws multi-national companies to us."

"Are there sufficient job opportunities here without tourism?" asked Stormy.

"Anyone who wants a job can get one. Literacy is 99% and

unemployment less than 1%," explained Linda. "Tourism is not entirely discouraged and St. Cats is well suited for it; with good climate, ample accommodations, and plentiful beaches, our island is both beautiful and accessible. No large hotels occupy the seaside property or block the ocean views."

They wandered through the city and its many parks. The parks were well maintained and similar to those of Paris and Rome in that they sported art, bistros, and expansive gardens to walk among.

It was early afternoon and most residents were still at work. The work day generally began at 8 a.m., broke from noon until 3 p.m. for lunch, and finally ended at 6 p.m. Thus, Linda and Stormy had the park almost to themselves. They picked a park bench that was out of the way on which to sit and rest their feet.

The park's public restroom stood nearby.

"Is that a restroom over there?" asked Stormy.

"Yes, the Men's is facing us and the Women's is on the other side."

Stormy excused herself and proceeded around the building to the ladies' side. Her footsteps echoed in the empty room. After she used the toilet she left the stall and went to the wash basin, bent over and turned on the tap to wash her hands.

An arm wrapped around her waist and a hand clasped over her mouth.

She started to kick and scream, but she was thrust up from the basin and her scream was muted by the reflection she saw in the mirror.

It was a vision of a face from her past, contorted by malice and hostility. The arm around her waist quickly moved up to her neck and in the mirror she saw the blade of a knife held a hair's breadth away from her throat.

CHAPTER FORTY

"HAPPY TO SEE ME, ARE YOU?" SNEERED Lars Conrad in Stormy's ear. "You thought you could just walk away after humiliating me in front of everyone and never face retribution?"

Stormy tried to speak, but could only mutter through his fingers.

"If you are trying to apologize, it is too late now. But, I'll give you a chance to speak," he said, pressing the knife against her throat. "I'm going to take my hand away from your mouth and turn you around slowly. If you even exhale too loudly, I will happily slit you from ear to ear."

As she turned, Stormy saw that the door to the washroom had been closed and bolted from the inside.

She tried to muster the courage to stay calm, despite her terror and dismay.

"Come on now, you had the audacity to announce your rejection of me publicly. Can't you speak to me in private?"

"I don't know what to say," she squeaked. "I will say anything you want to hear." Regaining some composure, she asked, "What do you want of me?"

"Now? Nothing is left but revenge. You will never be able

to pay for the way you treated me," he hissed. "Perhaps in your death I can find some comfort."

"Did you have anything to do with the attempts on my life?" she asked.

"Everything!"

Surprised, she continued, "You mean those people who tried to shoot me?"

"Yes. I even tried to run you down …"

"On Rodeo Drive?"

"Yes!"

"Oh my God, someone *was* trying to run me down. It was you! All those people … how did you convince them to try and kill me?"

"I explained that it was their patriotic duty."

"You did what?" Stormy's mind whirled as she thought of the events of the last several weeks. "My God, don't tell me that you are involved in the murders of those people on *The List*," she said, horrified.

"Inquisitive aren't we? I might as well tell you since you'll never be able to repeat it," he said.

His cold decisiveness made her painfully aware that he was going to kill her. *Keep him talking, she thought. Maybe Linda would miss me or someone would demand to use the restroom or a miracle would help …*

"It's not possible that one person could be the genesis of all the murders taking place," she faked disbelief, flattering him.

"It's possible and I am solely responsible—not for each act or even any one act, for that matter, but for the entirety of the operation."

He then went on to tell her about his scheme for revenge and the method by which he managed to effect its implementation. It was preposterous, yet it explained everything. Ross would have loved to be in possession of this information. Stormy thought it was a shame that she would probably not live to tell him.

Just then, the door rattled. A voice spoke in rapid French. *"'Alo, 'alo? S'il vous plait ouvre la porte, je dois aller au toilet."*

Lars inched the knife closer to Stormy's throat; he lay his finger over his lips to indicate silence.

The woman outside knocked loudly. *"Depechez vous-je'ne p'eux pas, plus attendre."*

"Tell her to go away," he hissed.

"I can't speak French," Stormy lied. She had recognized Linda's voice.

He silently slid the bolt back on the door latch and forced Stormy into a stall near the back with him.

They waited.

Someone entered and took a seat in the stall near the front. Stormy knew it had to be Linda. But what could she do?

Linda used the toilet, flushed, and exited the stall. The washroom door swung open and closed as she left.

Lars pushed Stormy out of the stall, still holding the knife at her throat. They stood in the middle of the room, facing the mirrors. "Goodbye, you little bitch," he hissed, and she felt the muscles in his arm tighten as he began to draw the knife across her neck.

Blackness spotted Stormy's vision and, as she felt herself sagging in his arms, she seemed to hear the sound of a champagne bottle being opened.

CHAPTER FORTY-ONE

STORMY HAD FAINTED AND WAS COMING TO by the time I arrived, which was only minutes from when Karl called. He told me he would explain the details later, but that Stormy was in need of me and that Lars was dead.

Lars's body was still in the washroom, lying cold in a pool of blood.

Linda and Stormy were seated on a park bench across from the facility.

"Stormy," I called out as I approached her.

She looked up, saw me, and rushed to me gladly. I gathered her in my arms and she began sobbing softly. I guided her back over to the bench that Linda had now vacated and we sat down, close, facing one another.

"I almost died!" she said, and began pounding on my chest with her fists. "You said I would be safe! Was this another of your plans?"

I clutched her hands to keep her still and get her full attention. "Stormy, please listen to me," I said calmly. "This was not a plan. I had no idea you would be in any real danger."

"Then why did you have Karl follow us? Linda said that you told him to."

"I did it just to be extra cautious. Karl was on St. Cats anyway, I thought it wouldn't hurt to have him keep an eye on you." I sighed. "I would never deliberately put you in harm's way. I only wanted to help you relax and to give you a break from all the stress you have endured."

"Is … is Lars dead?"

"Very," I answered.

"I don't remember much …" She touched her head briefly.

"That's good," I suggested.

"I thought I heard a champagne cork pop, but it was Karl's gun, wasn't it?"

"Yes." I nodded. "Let's get you back to *Villa Mar.* You can get cleaned up and we can discuss this with everyone involved. OK?"

"OK," she consented.

CHAPTER FORTY-TWO

WE WERE ALL SEATED AROUND THE GREAT room in *Villa Mar.* I had assembled Linda and Sterling, the local Inspector of Police, and Karl. Stormy had just joined us, and we all fell silent as she entered the room.

I asked, "Are you up to this, Stormy?"

"Yes," she replied. It was easy to see, however, that the terror, and, with it, the anger that flooded into her, had yet to fade.

"Stormy, may I get you a brandy?" Linda asked.

"That would be nice," replied Stormy.

As Linda rose to get the brandy, the door to the hall opened and a man dressed in a dark suit, white shirt with red tie, and laced black shoes entered. His hair was buzzed close to the scalp.

"Allow me to present Mr. Smith, the diplomatic liaison for the American embassy," I explained.

Turning back to the others, I continued "Stormy told me the facts she learned from Lars Conrad and, as fantastic as they appear, they mesh with all our other information."

"But how did Karl know I was being held by Lars in the washroom?" asked Stormy.

"He didn't. At least, not at first," I said. "Linda approached

Karl who she knew was nearby and expressed concern about the length of time that you had been in the washroom," I reiterated the facts as they were given me by Karl and Linda. "They eavesdropped and heard a male voice. Becoming suspicious, Karl and Linda devised a plan whereby Karl could get into the restroom. The plan depended heavily upon Linda being cool under pressure. Linda went into her French Lady act. They heard the bolt slide open, so Linda waited a few moments and eased the door open. Seeing no one outside the stalls, she and Karl entered and hid themselves in a stall, much the way Lars had done earlier. Linda proceeded to take a seat and use the bathroom to maintain their cover. Then Linda exited the washroom, leaving Karl hidden in the stall. When Lars pushed Stormy out of the stall and started to cut her throat, Karl shot Lars from behind."

"It's a shame we couldn't have taken him alive, but it appeared at the time that there was no other appropriate action I could have taken without further endangering Stormy," Karl said.

"Jolly right," piped up the inspector. "However, I still cannot connect all the dots in this bloody affair."

"It was a very devious plot indeed," offered Sterling.

Most of those standing grunted their agreement, but Mr. Smith stood mute.

"The most difficult item to get a grasp on was motive," I said. "We were all wondering what the killer's motive was for targeting Stormy," I added. "That quest was occluded by the multiple and apparently random acts of terror against a large group of people to which she had close association. The lines between acts against her and the group as a whole became blurred."

"It was not until we learned that Stormy was not on *The List* and made a full disclosure of her relationship with Lars, that the real motive began to appear and Lars become a suspect" interjected Karl.

"He also had a grudge against the others," Stormy reminded us.

"True," I nodded. "Even so, it was beyond belief that a crime of revenge would take on such proportions."

"Even granting Mr. Conrad the divisiveness and cunning of his scheme, how could anyone put in motion such an undertaking?" asked Mr. Smith.

"Timing and stupidity," I declared.

"You are not claiming he was stupid, are you?" retorted Mr. Smith.

"No, not Lars. The stupidity was of those who set up the perfect *cause dé jur.* Their inane quest to, once again, arbitrarily exempt themselves from estate and transfer taxes. Coincidentally this coincided with his personal agenda."

"He was never one to miss an opportunity of any sort," Stormy added.

"Ross, can you explain how Lars persuaded so many people to commit the callous murders of so many innocent people?" Sterling asked.

"I can only speculate. They were obviously malcontents and psychotics, and they were motivated by the largeness of their small acts. They were told, as we well know, that over a trillion dollars was being held by only five hundred people—or so, if you consider only families. These few families own more assets than ninety percent of all Americans.

"They also knew that, due to the near eminent upcoming changes in estate tax laws (the pending legislation), these families would be able to pass on their wealth to their heirs tax free. We're not just talking about the family farm here; but billions and billions of dollars. Lars convinced his followers that this enormous transfer of wealth marked the beginning of an aristocracy in America. Aristocracy is a concept repugnant to the majority of Americans and was one of the reasons for the American Revolution, and so it was an easy task to sell the murder of these modern day aristocrats to his chosen.

"But that alone was not sufficient motivation. The kicker, as they say, was that killing those wealthy Americans before the new tax law went into effect meant that the deceased would be subject to the old estate tax law. So now we understand the references to a deadline. The proponents of the change in the estate tax laws had inadvertently declared an open season on themselves.

"Under the current law, about to be repealed, theoretically, about one-half of the 1 trillion dollars could go into the U.S. Treasury. Almost enough to repair our roads and bridges or pay down the deficit," I concluded.

"Diabolical as it was, it had romance to some," agreed Mr. Smith.

"That brings us to the reason the Inspector has discretely disposed of the investigation of Mr. Lars Conrad and the reason for this meeting," I said.

"Which is?" asked Stormy.

"Try and let this storm blow over. There have been few killings of late and apparently the zeal as well as the perpetrators has diminished. Lars is gone and this thing will die a natural death, unless we breathe new life into it by making all of this public."

"Remember," Linda interjected, "that these are mostly the very same people who promoted the pickle they are now in."

"But now we need to be the adult and give this whole episode as decent burial as soon possible." I said.

"Agreed." chimed in everybody.

CHAPTER FORTY-THREE

"I GUESS THAT ENDS MY PROTECTIVE custody," lamented Stormy. After everyone had left the meeting and gone their separate ways Stormy and I went back to *Sea Witch*. We were having coffee in my office.

"Do you want it to end?" I asked.

"Not really," she admitted. "But if I no longer need it …"

"I'm still very uneasy about your situation," I admitted. "There are some things that I can't put to rest about this affair."

"You think we had an affair?" she smiled and said jokingly.

"I wish," I answered.

"You never expressed your wish."

"I never had time."

"And I do not have time," she said. "I must attend to business that has been ignored for too long …"

"I know, but even though the threat level is low, I have asked Karl to have some of his men keep an eye on you."

"I guess it can't hurt," she said.

"Well. I'm going to say goodnight and goodbye to you now. I have to leave early and I'll be gone before you get up.

Will you come back to see me when you have taken care of your affairs?"

"Do you want me to?" she asked, seeming only a little surprised and mostly pleased.

"Yes, I do."

CHAPTER FORTY-FOUR

STORMY HAD COMPLETED HER TASKS BACK in the States and began thinking more and more about Ross; missing him actually, she admitted to herself.

She couldn't get over a nagging sense of intruding on the lives and relationships between Ross and Dr. Nel Benet. Even though neither one seemed to mind, she needed more.

She decided the only way she could see Ross again was if she saw Nel first.

Stormy placed a call to Dr. Benet's clinic and after being told to hold for a moment she heard her come on the line.

"Stormy, is that you?"

"Yes Dr. Benet, I ..."

"What happened to Nel? Why are you getting all formal on me? Did I piss you off while you were here or is it something else?"

"No, nothing like that ... Nel, I, uh... need to see you."

"Why, have you become an adolescent with a neurological problem?"

"No," said Stormy as she unconsciously smiled, "it's about ..."

"I know what it's about; get yourself on one of your fancy jets, get down here and we'll talk about him."

"Thanks," Stormy said and gently laid down the receiver.

That night Stormy had her relief pilot fly her to Palm Beach, Florida in her Hawker where she transferred in the morning to a smaller jet for the short hop to Amelia Cay aboard her recently purchased new light jet.

Nel was waiting as the HondaJet taxied to a stop and Stormy stepped out to meet her.

"Come on, Stormy, I've got lunch laid out on the veranda."

They walked in silence to the table and sat down. As they picked up their napkins and began to eat, Nel said, "Stormy, I must apologize on behalf of Ross and myself for our conduct in keeping our former marriage secret from you."

Stormy began to speak but Nel cut her off with a wave of her hand and said, "Hear me out, please. We don't normally expose our former lives to outsiders. We jealously guard our secret because we have moved on and don't want our current lives complicated by our past lives."

"You mean; *the lives you could live only in your dreams?"*

Nel looked with surprise and asked, "Where in the world did you hear that?"

Stormy, embarrassed at what she had said, meekly replied, "Uh, Mike told me."

"You know Mike always did understand Ross and me; that's probably not a bad description."

"Really?" Stormy said with relief.

"True," replied Nel. "Ross and I loved each other and have a deep respect of one another; but we always wanted something else."

"We always wanted to become our dream personas. You know like Diana Prince is secretly Wonder Woman and Don Diego's alter ego is Zorro."

"But," Stormy intently said, "you already were Wonder Woman and Zorro."

"Yes, but we could not change back into Don Diego and Diane Prince. Do you know how much pressure it is to constantly be Wonder Woman? For me, on call 24/365 and always a child near death with little I could do. The strain was overwhelming. Same for Ross; always championing the underdog, not always winning, but always in battle."

"Weren't there some rewards?"

"Not really. Not genuine ones. We could win the battles, but never the war."

"I won't deny that we reaped huge amounts of money for our efforts, but I am sure a person of your wealth has learned that if you have plenty of money, it loses its importance."

"Unless money is the way you keep score, but I never really thought of it that way," answered Stormy.

"Well, we just wanted to become Don Diego and Diana, so to speak and that requires us to keep our past a secret. For instance, if everyone knew Clark Kent was Superman, poor old Clark could never get any rest or freedom."

"So why didn't the two of you just …"

"Run off together?"

"Yes."

"Our dream lives have different wants and purposes. Ross couldn't manage here on this island any more than I could handle the seclusion of the sea."

"How come?"

"Let's just say, women watch *Oprah* and men watch *How It's Made.*"

"So you and Ross …"

"Have a deep abiding respect for each other and share a common concern for each other's well-being."

"So …"

"So, go to Ross, but don't expect more than you get and take all that he will give."

"Nel," Stormy leaned closer and said, "You are an amazing woman."

"Yea, I'm a little older too, now run along and do something foolish."

CHAPTER FORTY-FIVE

I WAS SITTING AT MY USUAL SPOT AT THE bar playing Knock with Locks; something I had been doing a lot of lately. I was about to call it another day when I heard a soft voice in my ear ask, "Are you here alone, Captain?"

I turned and pulled her to me. "Not anymore, sailor," I murmured, and kissed her.

Two men dressed as Jewish Rabbis, apparently on sabbatical, watched Ross and Stormy intently.

They turned to each other. "Isn't that cute, Tom?" one of them remarked.

"Yes it is, John," the other replied.

CHAPTER FORTY-SIX

WHEN ROSS PULLED STORMY TO HIM AND kissed her at the bar, Locks was not the only one surprised. She was shocked but pleased to let the kiss linger until Ross pulled back and suggested they go to *Casa Tango.*

During their time aboard *Sea Witch,* Ross had told Stormy about his house at Elizabeth Isle. It seemed that everything in the Caribbean has a name attached to it. Hence, *Casa Tango.*

The two leisurely walked the same path they had hastily taken before, only now having the luxury to enjoy the view and each other's company. Stormy could hardly remember the terror she had felt when she first realized that she was being hunted.

It seemed a lifetime ago. A life apart from the one she now occupied and liked.

Stormy and Ross detoured from the path that led to *Sea Witch* and headed toward *Casa Tango.*

The house was built on a high bluff overlooking *Sea Witch*'s berth and the Atlantic Ocean beyond. The other side of the house faced the Caribbean Sea.

They walked up a set of wide steps to a large veranda and

a grand center foyer that continued through the house to the veranda on the opposite side.

Ross called out to someone named Mattie and spoke to her in a creole French dialect.

"Who are you talking to?" Stormy asked.

"Mattie, the cook," he replied. "We are just in time to add your name to the pot for supper."

"How wonderful!" Stormy exclaimed. "What about my luggage?"

"Locks will take care of everything," Ross said. "Why don't I fix you up with a drink and you can wander the house. By the time you complete the tour, your things will be in your room. You can then refresh yourself from your trip before dinner."

Stormy grinned. "That sounds perfect. What will you be doing in the meantime?"

"I need a few minutes in my office, and then I'll clean up and meet you on the veranda to watch the sunset before dinner. Why don't you have a drink?"

"What sort of drink?" Stormy wondered aloud.

"Your choice," Ross replied.

"Why don't you surprise me?" she requested.

"I thought you might say that," said Ross, signaling to a young boy in a white waiter's jacket who had appeared as if out of nowhere.

Damn, she thought, *how do they keep doing that?*

Within a minute, the boy returned with a tall glass filled with ice and a bright red cocktail, topped off with a wedge of pineapple, a cherry, and a paper umbrella.

"I know that's a little on the cutesy side, but how better to welcome you to the tropics than with an Elizabeth Isle Mai-Tai?" Ross said as Stormy took the concoction from the lad.

"If you need directions, all the housekeepers speak English. I'll see you here as promised, in an hour or so." With that, Ross walked away toward his office.

Stormy began her tour of *Casa Tango.*

The house was super tropical. That is to say, it incorporated all of the nuances evolved by people building and living in these latitudes for hundreds of years. The house was constructed of teak, walnut, and other hardwoods, which were left their natural colors and had aged beautifully. It had a thatched palapa roof to complete the tropical design.

The house had spectacular views which could be seen from the wide expanse of the veranda that completely surrounded the house, or from inside the house by merely opening any of the large plantation shutters that made up the exterior walls. The whole thing was situated atop a bluff that was landscaped with manicured lawns and gardens worthy of a villa in Italy.

There were living rooms, libraries, breakfast rooms, studios, formal and casual dining rooms, an office, an outdoor and indoor kitchen, four VIP bedroom suites and, a grand master bedroom suite. In addition, rich, flowing, colorful fabrics covered or accented every room.

No wonder he had declined to describe it to her before. Words could not convey the beauty or the feeling of comfort and simple elegance emitted by *Casa Tango.*

CHAPTER FORTY-SEVEN

I MET STORMY ON THE VERANDA AS PROMISED and we settled into huge, thickly-cushioned teak chairs with wide arms that negated the need for side tables. Our chairs abutted each other, facing toward the horizon where the sun was about to set over the Caribbean. I reached over and grasped her hand; we sat in silence as the sun bid *adieu* to our side of the earth in order to give light to those awaiting the sunrise.

Afterward, we ate in the informal dining room, at a table–clothed dining table set with china and silver service. Dinner was much simpler and more pleasing than the extravaganza we'd had at St. Cats when this all began. We dined on fresh fruits and sea foods all prepared in a healthy manner; yet well-seasoned and artfully presented.

Ross wore an off-white linen suit that had obviously been custom made, with a pink Egyptian cotton shirt, French cuffs, and cufflinks made of old Spanish pieces of eight. The suit was complemented by a silk tie and simple but luxurious leather sandals.

Stormy wore a red strapless cocktail dress, fitted at the waist, with a pleated skirt that extended to just above her knees, red strappy sandals, and a glistening diamond necklace with matching earrings.

The meal was finished without mentioning the affair that had brought them together, but "The Rule" was suspended prior to dessert.

"What has happened since I left? I have been so occupied and, I might add, in such a rush to return, that I neglected to keep up," asked Stormy.

I reviewed the news stories of the past several weeks.

I told her the cadre of assassins that Lars Conrad had inspired quickly fell apart as their targets disappeared, their leadership waned and their attorney's fees ended. Being amateurs, their ability to act was based solely on opportunity and so the hunters gave up the hunt.

"It appears to be over, just as we predicted," I said.

Stormy and I were happy it was over and were glad to assume that she was no longer in danger.

We had just finished dessert when a young man, different from the one who had served Stormy her drink, approached me and whispered in my ear.

I rose, placed my napkin in my chair, and said, "There's a call from Sterling on my office phone, I should probably take it. I'll only be a minute."

Stormy sat, watching the ocean for only a minute, and then decided she would not wait for Ross to return. She found him seated at his desk chair in an office decorated very much like his office on *Sea Witch*. She crept up behind him as he replaced the phone in its cradle, leaned over and put her arms around him, and kissed him on his ear.

He swiveled around and sat her in his lap. Then he kissed her in the way she had wanted him to kiss her since the moment she first saw him.

He picked her up as he rose from his chair and carried her to his bedroom.

CHAPTER FORTY-EIGHT

TOM AND JOHN SAT IN A DARK BOOTH IN THE back of a dingy bar in an old part of Brooklyn, nursing whiskeys and watching football on the overhead TV. John could hear Tom's side of the conversation with their client.

"No, I can't absolutely guarantee that she will be available," Tom said reassuringly into the phone. "But I can guarantee that we will be ready and able to perform."

After a moment's pause, he replied, "You won't let us do anything now, when we have the chance. How can we assure you we'll be able to kill her on the date you want? That is a circumstance over which we have no control." After another pause, Tom continued, "It's very difficult to maintain access to her without spooking her. She might recognize us, after a time."

"Yes, we know it can't be done until the law changes, but …"

Tom listened again for a moment. "You know what happened last time—we are lucky she reappeared." Tom continued, "Look if you can't give us a date and if the date is now soon …"

He was cut off by loud, angry words. "Okay, okay," he said,

"I understand. John and I will come up with a plan, but this is going to cost you double, at least, plus all expenses. By the way, it would be best if you sent another advance now, and be prepared to provide any services or transportation we need."

Tom nodded to the phone. As he hung up, he said to John, "Our client is getting panicky. We need a new plan—our client has problems that are just now becoming clear. Apparently the law can be changed by Congress anytime they can reach an agreement on it."

"We need to be able to get to her at a moment's notice," said John.

"Yeah, we need to put her into cold storage."

CHAPTER FORTY-NINE

I COULDN'T REMEMBER WHEN I HAD LAST felt so young.

Stormy had taken on a new persona as well. With the worry of imminent death behind her, she greeted each day with the joy of being alive and the world as if she had just seen it for the first time.

Drifting off to sleep with her at night was enhanced only by the joy of finding her next to me when I awoke in the morning. We often languished blissfully together in the space between sleep and awareness, and only arose in order to begin another day together.

I finally admitted to Stormy that I owned Elizabeth Isle and had made it into an adult playground for my personal pleasure.

Since we had reunited we had done nothing significant, yet we lived each day to its fullest. Our days were diverse and there was an endless number of diversions to occupy our time. Some days we would shoot skeet or trap, or dive, or just swim in the lagoon. Occasionally I would take her on a picnic to adjacent cays, where we would fish or walk the beaches.

"I want to go shopping," she said one morning as we finished breakfast.

"Do we need anything?" I asked.

"No, I just want to go shopping," she repeated.

"OK," I said, "I realize that we haven't been off island since you arrived. I know it has been several weeks, but it seems like only days to me."

"I just want to keep up with the fashions and styles and buy some pretty things," she said persuasively.

"That part I like."

"What part?"

"The part about you in pretty things," I said.

"You are a pig," she said, laughing.

I oinked playfully. "Get ready and I'll make all the arrangements for you."

"Aye, aye, Captain," she said as she walked out of the room.

I took a swat at her butt as she passed.

"Be a good boy until I get back and I'll put on a fashion show for you," she teased.

"I'll be waiting."

I summoned *Sea Witch's* Captain to the house and, as I waited, I thought to myself how pleasant my life had become since Stormy's arrival.

"Captain," I said as he approached the porch, "I want you to take the center-console and escort Mrs. Richter to Victoria Island. Take along another hand and do not let her out of your sight."

Even though it seemed that the killing had abated, I still harbored uneasiness in the back of my mind.

CHAPTER FIFTY

"DAMN IT TO HELL, WHY DOES SHE ALWAYS have to go to the restroom?" Ross yelled at no one in particular and everyone in general. "Don't answer that, it was rhetorical," he continued.

He was pacing in front of the prefect's desk and several gendarmes, a secretary, and his captain and mate were crammed in the small office.

"Mr. Barr," the prefect of the gendarmes said, "once again, the only facts we have place her entering the restroom. No one claims to have seen her leave.

"Your captain was near the doorway and didn't leave until he grew worried and left to alert a nearby officer. The two returned to the facility, announced themselves, and searched the washroom. It was unoccupied at that time."

"There is a back door that exits onto a narrow alleyway behind the facility," added one of the gendarmes,

"We questioned everyone in this area; no one remembers seeing anyone matching her description," concluded the prefect and he added as an after-thought, "if she was taken off the island she would not be able to enter any other country."

"Why is that?" asked Ross.

"She probably didn't bother to take her passport with her for a shopping trip, no?"

"Right, she left it at *Casa Tango*."

"More importantly, we have issued an international BOLO. Customs and immigration checkpoints at all points of entry have her name."

Ross stopped pacing and fuming. He faced the group and said, "I apologize for my behavior. You have all done everything you could or that could be expected.

"Captain," he continued, "take me back to Elizabeth Isle. I have work to do."

CHAPTER FIFTY-ONE

THE TWO IMMIGRATION AGENTS WERE summoned to the airdrome at midmorning. Usually they met the incoming flights after dark.

"Well, this is nice," said one of the agents as they stood on the tarmac waiting for the jet to stop taxiing. "I had breakfast before I got the call and we should be finished before lunch."

"Is that all you think about—food?" the other responded, as the jet rolled to a stop.

"Not all … oh, there they are now."

The two men approached the jet as usual, awaiting delivery of yet another soul in great distress.

The port engine shut down and the cargo door began to open.

No one bothered to chock the wheels as was the usual case.

The ambulance parked next to the cargo door, also as usual. The door opened and lowered and there were the two attendants and a person on the gurney.

This time there was no life support equipment; only a sleeping woman, accompanied by two men in business suits. This was a departure from the norm, but not enough of a departure to cause concern. One of the suited men handed over papers for three. The officers checked the photos against their faces as an officer typed the three names into his handheld mobile unit to verify their status as being able to enter the country.

The two men accompanying her were very nonchalant about the whole affair.

Soon the screen lit up and the officer, assured that all was in order, returned the passports and nodded for them to pass.

The woman was loaded into the ambulance by the two attendants and the two men in suits got into the back with her.

As the ambulance drove off, one of the officers said, "That's the first lively looking one we have seen yet, I think."

"It is also the first patient not from the U.S."

"No?" mused the other.

"No, she had a French passport."

CHAPTER FIFTY-TWO

I CALLED KARL JONES AND MIKE BUTLER ON my way back to get the things that I would need for the upcoming trip. Mike would fly himself and Karl in Stormy's Hawker to Victoria Island, where we would meet.

Waiting for my friends and allies to arrive in the lobby of the Fixed Base Operator (FBO), I churned every piece of data I had collected since meeting Stormy over and over in my mind. I had never been completely satisfied that everything was accounted for, but I couldn't think of what I had missed.

I requested Karl's presence because Karl might have information I could use. I certainly could use his expertise, along with his other skills. And Mike was a longtime friend of both Stormy's and I; he might know something that he didn't even realize was important. Even in the face of the world wide BOLO I was sure that Stormy had somehow been taken off the island, and I needed the rapid access Mike's jet would give us if anybody learned of her whereabouts. Sterling would be in charge of operations on the island, in the event that I was wrong and she was still on the island. I saw the plane turning on final approach and walked outside to wait for it to taxi up to the ramp. The port engine shut down as the airstair lowered from the fuselage. I climbed the steps carrying my two bags. The door began to retreat as the port engine began spinning.

I was met by a steward who took the bags, and noticed a first officer, standing in the galley, whom I had previously met. Karl was right behind; he introduced me to two of his associates—Jim and Wayne. He said he would explain later why he brought them along.

Mike's voice came over the speaker. "We are beginning our take-off roll. Belt up, and I will be back there as soon as we clear departure control."

Within a few minutes, Mike exited the cockpit and the first officer entered and closed the door. Mike walked to the midsection of the main cabin, where the others were seated. He took a seat in a large, overstuffed leather chair similar to the one I was occupying. The seats could swivel or recline, and he turned his to face me and asked, "Well, what the hell is going on, Ross? I came as quickly as possible."

"I appreciate that, Mike; you too, Karl," I said, and I meant it. "I am at my wits end and need all the help … I should say that Stormy needs all the help she can get."

"I have briefed Mike on all that transpired since he last saw Stormy," said Karl.

"Obviously she has been kidnapped. The island is too small for her to have not turned up by now." I said.

"I let myself believe that there was no further danger to Stormy," I said, mournfully. "After all, she really was not on *The List* and the only person trying to do her harm was Lars Conrad, and he is dead. Once again I'm at a loss to understand who would want to hurt Stormy or why. But there is one item that still has not been answered, Karl. I don't know any details about your assignment to protect Stormy."

Karl responded, "Nor do I, as yet. We quit receiving our retainer soon after Lars Conrad was killed. No explanation was given and the entity's identity is still a mystery to us."

"Who would have a special interest in keeping her alive? And why?" asked Mike.

"What happened to Tom and John?" I asked Karl.

"I was curious about that myself. I made some inquiries and came up with nothing. They must have changed their identities," Karl said.

"How did your anonymous employer know that Stormy's life was in danger in the first place?" I wondered.

"It had to be someone who suspected that Lars Conrad still held a grudge against her and might act on it," Karl offered.

"The only people I know who kept up any association with Lars Conrad were her nephews," Mike said.

"What? Why?" I asked.

"It had something to do with some deal he got them into that went bad. They believed Lars had some money hidden away, and they were trying to locate it. The boys were hostile towards Lars, but I had the feeling they knew more about him than they let on."

"I think we should concentrate on trying to find out how her kidnappers got her off the island and where they have taken her," Karl said.

"I agree. I have a friend that has tracked every flight from Victoria Island since Stormy went missing, along with all possible connecting flights. Commercial flights are out—too public—so we only had to search for private or charter flights," Mike said

"Any luck yet?" I asked.

"Some. I have considerable contacts with the charter community, and I've come up with a few leads."

"And?" I asked.

CHAPTER FIFTY-THREE

"THERE WAS A CITATION III THAT LANDED and left Victoria Island within a two-hour time span during the time Stormy failed to reappear from the restroom," Mike said. "I thought it significant at first, so I tracked it as far as I was able."

"What did you find?" I urged.

"The flight terminated at George Bush International Airport in Houston, Texas (IAH), and apparently taxied to a hanger without an FBO.

"The hangar space can be rented by the month, day, or year with no questions asked. Apparently no one was around when the Citation III arrived. The aircraft was chartered without a crew by a company that exists only on paper. Payment was made in advance by cashier's check. The pilots filed a flight plan to Aruba with a fuel stop at Victoria Island. They didn't have to clear customs or immigration because no one entered the country. They used a self-serve fuel depot, paid in cash, and departed for Aruba."

Mike continued, "They could have snuck Stormy on board during refueling at Victoria. Once airborne, they declared a minor glitch in the on board avionics and cancelled Aruba as their destination and requested and received permission to change the flight plan to return to IAH for repairs.

"The plane is still in the hanger and the pilots are nowhere to be found."

"So, we lost their trail." I concluded.

"I have my people with pictures of Stormy checking all ground personnel at IAH and surrounding airports for anyone who might have seen her. That is where we are headed now," Mike said.

CHAPTER FIFTY-FOUR

WE LANDED AT MIKE'S BASE OF OPERATION at his hanger at IAH and used his large conference room as our headquarters. We then scoured all private flight records out of the area and gathered reports from Karl's people on the ground.

"I've called in all my favors," said Mike, "and Karl's people or mine have personally spoken with at least one crew member of every flight out of here during the twenty-four hours after the Citation III landed.

"No one remembers anyone matching Stormy's description."

"Another dead end," I lamented.

"Maybe not," Karl said, pursing his lips. "It's obviously a long shot, but one of my men talked with a mechanic who worked on the main gear of a G-3 that was eager to depart. The G-3 was configured as an air ambulance and while he was fixing the gear, the crew loaded a woman on a gurney. He could not see her face so he couldn't be sure it was Stormy."

Mike rose from his chair at the head of the conference table, strode over to another table, and picked up a file folder. "I have all the flight records on that G-3. I thought it odd that no matter where it departed from it always arrived at the same destination—a small private airstrip in Europe in the Alps. I checked with the lease manager of the aircraft, and he said the aircraft had been chartered for a six month period, beginning about three months ago. He also told me it was a bare charter—the lessee provided his own aircrew, medical personnel and maintenance. That was all he knew."

"I have resources in the area," said Karl. "My operatives will get to the bottom of this."

"Let's move out!" I said.

CHAPTER FIFTY-FIVE

WE WERE AIRBORNE WITHIN SEVERAL HOURS of receiving Karl's intel. We learned there was a private clinic near the airport that the G-3 frequented. That would explain why the plane was set up as an ambulance.

We learned nothing specific about the clinic, except that it had only been in operation about nine months, and it had no ties to any of the doctors or hospitals in the area.

The locals in the area were suspicious of the clinic because of the secrecy of its operations. We had no proof or tangible evidence that Stormy was there, but we were certain enough to risk possible incarceration to find out. Our strike force, as it was, consisted of me and Mike; and Karl and his two associates, Jim and Wayne.

Mike had equipped the Hawker with some special night vision equipment, not unlike what we had on *Sea Witch,* which was so good that we could see an object rising only one meter above sea level at over a mile. That, along with state-of-the-art GPS and other avionics, would allow us to land on the Alps strip at night without any runway lights.

We listed the airdrome in the Alps as one of our fuel stops on a flight plan to Rome, so we would not have to clear customs or immigration until we landed in Italy—hopefully after having retrieved Stormy from the mysterious clinic, if she was there.

We had been airborne for three hours since our last fuel stop and were nearing the airstrip. We were lucky—there were no clouds and an almost full moon, which glowed directly overhead.

With great skill and some luck, we touched down, stopping just short of the end of runway.

Karl and I immediately exited the Hawker and climbed into a waiting Peugeot Sedan and with a driver supplied by Karl. Jim and Wayne were burdened with large obviously heavy duffle bags, taken from the plane, and secured them in the trunk. They crowded in the sedan with us and we made our way up a curving, climbing, gravel one lane road to the clinic.

Mike taxied back down the runway to make ready for a hasty takeoff.

We were able to stay in contact with Mike via our two-way communication headsets. He was to leave us if we encountered conditions we could not manage.

We arrived at the entrance gate to the clinic around one a.m. The four of us exited the sedan and the driver made a U-turn positioning our car for a fast getaway if necessary. Jim and Wayne retrieved our weapons from the duffels. We were heavily armed with untraceable weapons we could ditch, but prayed there would be no need for violent action.

Surveillance of the area performed earlier by Karl's men had not revealed any special security measures; however, Jim approached the clinic under the ruse of being lost and needing directions, he was curtly and rudely turned away. We reconnoitered the building and grounds, which were lit only by landscape lighting. Each man had a portion of the premises to secure and we found nothing as well as no special security lights.

We made our way around to the back entrance single file. There was an old ambulance bay and doors that were no longer used. We quietly picked the lock on one of the rear doors and entered a dimly lit hallway one by one being careful to make as little noise as possible.

We found nothing but an old, out-of-date medical facility that had been neglected and then repainted and remodeled, but to no great extent. Wide swinging doors without locks lined the hallway, which was floored with small, white, octagon-shaped tiles. Most of the doors were partially open, and the faint glow of florescent lighting emitted from the rooms, spilling into the hallway.

Jim and Wayne took the left side and Karl and I took the right. We glanced into each room as we quietly made our way down the hall toward a pair of frosted glass doors that glowed from the light of the room within.

Each of the rooms we looked into along the way was furnished with a bed that held a patient surrounded by banks of medical equipment with lights that blinked dutifully. We had no time to investigate the rooms and continued down the hall.

We gathered by the double doors and, on my signal Jim and Wayne burst through the unlocked doors into the brightly lit room, which contained several desks, a table, chairs, and a kitchen counter with a sink and a large coffee urn on it. Karl and I came in on their heels.

The room was apparently used as a lounge or break room. Two male orderlies dressed in white uniforms jumped up from around a table near one end of the room almost upending it.

They stood facing us with a surprised and stunned look on their faces.

"Either of you speak English?" I shouted as we all trained our weapons on them.

"Yes," said one.

"Ja," the other.

"Who are you and what are you doing here?" asked the first one.

"We are looking for a friend," I replied. "Are you American?"

"Yes," he answered. "I speak English and Spanish. My name is Juan. And we don't know about your friend—we only work here to watch over the equipment until the day shift comes at seven a.m."

I walked over to where Juan stood and looking him straight in the eye, asked,

"Where are the doctors and nurses?"

"There are no doctors or nurses," he blurted, "at least not on our shift. There is at least one head doctor, but we have only met him once."

I shoved a picture of Stormy in front of his face. He paled and turned to the other orderly. "I told you when those thugs showed up with that woman that I did not like it," he said.

"Shut up, you fool!" ordered the one with broken English.

Then he turned to me and said, "Ve vas only taking orders. They said she krazy and poot her in von of the old padded cells used ven this vas loony bin."

"Where are the men now?" I demanded.

"They are sleeping in the old caretaker's quarters and are supposed to drive to Vienna and fly to the States tomorrow," said Juan.

"And what were you supposed to do with the woman?"

"Nothing, we were told nothing. We were hired only to maintain the medical equipment. After the woman arrived we decided to quit at the first opportunity."

"All right, Juan! Show us where the woman is being held. Jim, you come with me. Karl, you and Wayne take the other orderly and collect the two sleeping thugs. OK?"

"Sure thing," said Karl as they departed for the caretaker's quarters with the orderly in the lead.

Juan led Jim and I down a stairway to a poorly-lit hall lined with white metal doors on each side. Each door had a small square glass window imbedded with what looked like chicken wire that was held in place by a riveted metal frame. Each door had a large deadbolt lock. All the doors were open save one.

"She is in that one," the orderly said, pointing to the closed door.

"Give me the key!" I demanded. He took a large skeleton key off a nail hidden behind one of the open doors and handed it to me. I made Juan back up to give me room to open the door. I went to the door. The cell was dark and I couldn't see through the glass window. I eased the key into the lock, turned the bolt, and swung the door open.

I used the Zeon lithium powered flashlight at my belt to search around the cell. It was empty of furniture save for a metal cot screwed to the wall. A figure lay on the cot, with blankets pulled up over its head. The person began to move, and Stormy's face appeared from under the covers. She covered her eyes against the flashlight's bright blast, and I quickly lowered my arm. I rushed to her and took her in my arms.

"Who are you?" she asked in a slurred, drugged voice. She trembled.

"It's me, Stormy—Ross. I have come to get you."

"Ross? Ross? Oh Ross!" she cried as she buried her head in my chest. "Where am I? How did you find me?"

"Later," I whispered in her ear as I picked her up from the cot and carried her up the stairs into the large room. She was heavily sedated and seemed to reel in and out of consciousness as I held her. I laid her on a couch near the far wall. She dozed off again.

Standing in the room beside Karl, Jim, and the orderly were two men handcuffed together.

"Ross, I would like to introduce you to Tom and John," said Karl.

CHAPTER FIFTY-SIX

STORMY HAD GOTTEN UP FROM THE COUCH and now sat quietly at the table, drinking her third cup of coffee.

Jim and Wayne had placed our prisoners at a table across the room. Karl and I were out of earshot at one of the desks, where we could speak privately, in order to discuss what changes we should adopt now that we had discovered Tom and John.

We were about to ask Mike for his input over our comm set when we heard a loud scream from down the hall where we had first entered the building.

I looked around the room for Stormy and, to my chagrin, saw that she was absent.

Before I could rise from behind the desk, I heard from down the hall the loud sound of objects falling and glass breaking and running footsteps.

I ran to the hallway with Karl close behind. We saw a figure exit a room and run into another room directly across the hall. This was followed by the sound of a loud crash and breaking and falling equipment, followed by more loud screams from Stormy.

I raced to the doorway and turned on the lights to find an overturned bed with Stormy lying underneath a form in a hospital gown, both tangled in wires, medical equipment, hoses, and lots of plastic tubing that leaked and pumped various colors of fluids across the worn and stained linoleum floor.

Stormy was alternately screaming and thrashing about; trying to free herself from the debris she was caught in.

Karl and I cleared away enough of the mess to lift her up by her armpits and carry her into the hall, where she stopped screaming and began to sob.

Through her sobs she kept repeating, "They are all dead! They are all dead! They are all dead!"

I took her by the shoulders and gently shook her and made her focus her eyes on mine. "Who is dead, Stormy?" I asked quietly.

"All of them," she replied, her sobs now quieting, her composure returning to something similar to normal.

"Who are all of them?" I asked again, still in a quiet voice.

"I believe I can answer for Stormy," I heard Karl call out from an adjacent room. "It seems that these rooms are occupied by a number of embalmed bodies, all attached to some sort of modified life support system. At a glance, it appears to be typical life support equipment, but actually it is equipment meant only to preserve their bodies. They are all dead!"

"That is what I was trying to say," Stormy explained. "I started feeling better after several cups of coffee and I noticed you two in deep conversation, so I decided to have a look around.

"I went into one of the rooms, turned on the overhead

lights and went over to the side of the bed. I put my hand on the exposed hand of the person … body … lying in the bed. It was cold as ice! I pulled down the covers to see what was wrong, and, well you can see for yourself."

I looked at the body—the abdomen had ripped open and its intestines were exposed. I clamped down on a slight feeling of nausea.

"I was so startled that I knocked over the stand holding the I.V. bottle and ran into the room across the hall to get away. I tripped on something as I ran into the darkened room and fell headlong into a bed, which toppled over on me, dragging with it the occupant on the bed and all the medical equipment attached.

"That is where you and Karl came in," she concluded.

Karl motioned me to yet another room down the hall. Before joining him, I took Stormy back to the break-room and left her under the supervision of Jim and Wayne.

"I'm going to check the other rooms with Karl," I told Stormy. "Please wait here for a few minutes and I will have you taken to the plane, where you can take a bath, clean up, and change clothes."

"OK," she said weakly, her emotions having been drained.

Returning to Karl, I found not one but three figures in three different beds, all plugged to their respective machines, which busily pumped, whined, and monitored their own functions.

"What the hell?" I mused as Karl verified that each figure was actually the body of a person who was now stone cold dead and fairly well preserved.

"What the hell! is right," muttered Karl. "Let's check the other rooms."

By our count there were thirty-one bodies in all. This number was verified by the two orderlies, who admitted that their job was simply to keep the equipment functioning.

"What do you think you are doing?" I demanded.

Juan replied, "The doctor told us when we met him that this was a life extension experiment. He said that these people, or their families, had paid to have them preserved until a cure or future medical advancements made it possible for them to be revived. He said the process was not unlike when people have their bodies frozen in an attempt to defeat death.

"We became nervous when these two thugs showed up with the woman several days ago," he gestured to Tom, John, and Stormy. "They locked her up downstairs. We were hired to help maintain a legitimate clinic," he said proudly, "not babysit for kidnappers. We decided to quit at the first opportunity, but you arrived before the opportunity presented itself."

"I can appreciate that," I said, nodding.

I got Mike on the comm line and let him know that I was sending Stormy to him with Karl's driver, in the Peugeot. I also let him know that we were going to delay our departure until the next shift arrived, so we could question them as well.

Then I asked Juan if he had any way to contact the head doctor in case of an emergency.

He replied "What emergency? They're all dead! But," he continued, "there is a number we use to report if the next shift is late or to order supplies that might be needed for the coming day."

"Call it!" I ordered. "And tell whomever answers that the doctor must come immediately because the woman is sick."

"What if they ask what's wrong with her?" he asked.

"Just tell whoever that she is non-responsive and looks ill."

He picked up the receiver, looked at it, paused and then dialed the number and told the person on the other end what I had instructed him to say. He waited for a response. "Yes sir," he said, and replaced the receiver in its cradle.

Turning to me, he said, "That was the doctor, himself. He said he would come immediately."

We offered the two orderlies a deal. If they agreed to wait in the caretaker's cabin until we left, we would let them go and not involve them in our investigations. They agreed and we locked them in to assure that they wouldn't try to leave early.

Tom and John were locked up in one of the cells downstairs before Stormy left for the plane. We planned on taking them with us, but hadn't yet decided what to do about the doctor.

Karl, Jim, Wayne, and I took positions around the front door and awaited the doctor's arrival.

We heard a car approach and park in the driveway. The car door opened and closed and the sound of footsteps approached the front door. As the doorknob turned and the door began to open, I jerked it the rest of the way open. Along with it came a surprised, middle aged, short, overweight male in a doctor's smock. He was pale and prematurely gray, with a white beard and a puffy face.

He stood, mouth agape, and stared at the four armed strangers that surrounded him.

CHAPTER FIFTY-SEVEN

"DON'T ASK US WHAT WE ARE DOING HERE, Doctor," I said. "The question is, what in the hell are you doing here?"

He stood silent.

"Don't be coy. We have gone through the entire clinic and there is nothing you can hide from or lie your way out of."

"I have done nothing wrong," he asserted in unaccented English.

"Then tell us what you have done," I demanded.

"These are life extension experiments, all authorized by the families of the deceased and completely legal," he explained, with a confidence he certainly did not feel.

"You can do nothing to me," he went on, "and now you must leave."

"What sort of life extension were you going to perform on the woman?" I inquired.

He clammed up and lowered his head.

"We have talked with the two gentlemen who brought her in and we know of your involvement in her kidnapping and holding her prisoner here," I lied.

With that pronouncement, he deflated.

"You know that every occupant of those rooms down the hall are dead, do you not, doctor …? Uh, are you really a doctor?"

"Yes, I am Doctor Klein. And yes, they are clinically dead, but, as I told you, we are trying to preserve their bodies so in the future they might be brought back to life."

"I would leave the resurrection gig up to someone more competent. Say, God for instance." I smirked. "And, one more thing," I added with a sudden inspiration. "Despite how it looks *none* of these people are really dead, are they, Doctor?"

CHAPTER FIFTY-EIGHT

THE DOCTOR TURNED AND BEGAN RUNNING out of the clinic. His sudden departure caught us all off guard, but Jim ran him to ground before he could get more than twenty paces away.

"I guess that answers some of our questions," I remarked.

"Jim, take him downstairs and lock him up, far enough away from the other two to prevent them from conversing with each other, and stay there to make sure that they do not," I requested.

After a conversation with Mike and Karl, in which I learned that Stormy had arrived at the plane and was showering, we agreed on a plan.

We definitely needed to get the hell out of there as quickly as possible. We also needed time to interrogate our three unexpected "guests." I had a comprehensive idea of what was happening at the clinic, but I wanted to confirm my theory and obtain solid evidence that would prove it beyond a doubt.

To accomplish this, I needed to take our suspects along with us to a safe and undisclosed location so they could be interrogated.

We decided to fly to our scheduled fuel stop outside of

Rome with everyone on board. Due to our good planning and foresight, we had a G-4 standing by in Rome as a backup aircraft. It had officially been used to deliver a trade delegation to Rome from St. Catherine. The passengers had deplaned, cleared customs and immigration, and were scheduled to return to St. Catherine by commercial flight three days hence.

Our flight plan identified Rome as our destination but, once airborne, we would change Rome to a refueling stop and amend our flight plan to make our final stop St. Catherine.

We sent Jim, along with our three unwilling passengers, to the airstrip in the Peugeot with Karl's driver. Wayne, Karl, and I followed in the doctor's car. We released the two orderlies from the caretaker's cabin as promised and they took off immediately.

We all boarded the Hawker and placed Tom, John, and the doctor in restraints in the rear, with Jim and Wayne watching over them with stun guns. Stormy, having completed her bath and wardrobe change, lay exhausted on the forward couch with Karl seated across from her. I took the co-pilot seat.

Mike had found the switch for the runway lights and Karl's driver would flip them on for our departure and off after we rotated.

Before we were wheels up, both Stormy and Karl were asleep.

It was a short flight to the airport outside of Rome where we were to refuel and switch to the G-4. Since no one was planning to enter the country, it was not necessary to present papers to anyone for inspection or clearance. While the Hawker was refueling, Jim, Wayne, and the doctor, with Tom and

John in tow, made the short trip from our plane to the G-4 across the black tarmac, and departed on the return flight to St. Catherine, as previously scheduled.

Mike had called Sterling earlier and arranged for the G-4 to land and taxi directly to an official secure hanger at St. George, bypassing normal entry procedures and since the entire flight had been flagged diplomatic from the start, and presumably only the pilots were on board, this was not a problem.

Once in the hanger, our three detainees would be transported to another secure facility where they would rest and await interrogation. Karl, Mike, Stormy, and I would also arrive in St. Catherine at the St. George airport, but would be properly cleared into the country by customs.

On the flight from Rome to St. Cats, I got on the air phone and managed to make an anonymous phone call to the local authorities near the clinic. All I told them was that the place seemed abandoned and there were a whole lot of corpses up there.

I activated the pilot to co-pilot intercom and said to Mike over the headset: "I can't wait to see what the news media is going to do with this discovery!"

CHAPTER FIFTY-NINE

THE FLIGHTS TO ST. CATS WERE UNEVENTFUL, and both arrived within a few minutes of each other. Our "guests" were delivered to their location, and the four of us went to *Villa Mar,* where we took long baths and went directly to bed.

The next morning Karl and Sterling were awaiting the rest of us when Stormy and I arrived, followed shortly by Linda, and then Mike.

While we were being served breakfast, we discussed the recent events. Stormy related how someone had covered her face with gauze soaked in something that rendered her helpless. Her next cogent memory was of being in the cell, and then our arrival. She never saw the doctor and only vaguely remembered visions of Tom and John. She could offer no additional motive for this latest attack on her or why she was kidnapped.

Neither the BBC nor any other news concern had yet to break a story involving the clinic in the Alps.

Our general consensus was that there would be a delay in releasing any information by the authorities until they could deliver a coherent story to the press and try to avoid looking stupid.

Good luck, I thought.

CHAPTER SIXTY

I WAS ALONE IN AN INTERROGATION ROOM with Doctor Klein. He was seated at a bare table facing the obligatory one-way glass, behind which Karl and Mike watched and listened.

The doctor looked terrible; he reeked of fear and uncertainty.

"Look," I said, "you know you are the designated scapegoat in this matter. Your only salvation is that we are not sworn officers of the law and you are not in official custody yet!"

He regained some fortitude and reiterated his mantra. "I was doing nothing illegal."

"I think we have had about enough of that bullshit," I retorted. "You are a willing accomplice in the kidnapping of Mrs. Richter and her transportation across international boundaries. The penalties range from life imprisonment, without parole, to death."

"Or else?" he prompted.

"I can't say for sure until I am convinced of your complete honesty and the full divulgence of your involvement in this affair. It further depends upon the depth of your involvement."

He blinked.

"I am willing to give you the benefit of the doubt because

I don't think your participation involved the intentional or negligent deaths of anyone. Am I right?" I questioned.

"I swear I never knew Mrs. Richter or anyone else alive would ever be involved," he stated forcefully.

"You do admit that your 'patients' were already dead when they arrived at the clinic?"

"Oh, dear God, yes! They were quite dead even before they were put on the plane for the trip to the clinic." he continued.

Now for the pregnant question. "Did you really expect any of them to be revived at a future date?"

"No. What the future held for them was the death they had so far been denied."

CHAPTER SIXTY-ONE

"I'LL BE DAMNED," MIKE SAID, REPEATING the doctor's words, "'The death they had so far been denied.' Ross was right all along. He knew it all involved the pending estate tax law changes."

Ross left the interrogation room and joined Karl and Mike in the observation portion. Looking through the one-way glass at the Doctor, Mike asked me," How does this involve Stormy?"

"I'll tell you for sure as soon as I get Tom or John to admit who their employer is. I also suspect they have numerous other clients and lots of unfinished business."

"Do you think they will tell?" asked Karl.

"I am certain of it," I replied. "There is no need for your continued presence. Give me a couple of hours and I will meet everyone back at *Villa Mar* and explain everything."

They left, and I had Tom and John brought into the interrogation room.

I was not alone.

"OK, you two," I began. "You have only one way out of certain death or life imprisonment, and the gentleman standing next to me is it. Allow me to introduce Mr. Smith."

CHAPTER SIXTY-TWO

"OK, SHERLOCK," QUIPPED STORMY, "TELL us mere mortals what happened."

We were all seated comfortably around the great room at *Villa Mar*, each with drinks of our choice graciously provided by our hosts, Linda and Sterling, who were both present. Also in attendance were Mike, Karl, and the inspector who assisted with Stormy's first washroom incident.

There was a knock on one of the double doors to the great room. It opened and a gentleman entered whom all had seen but to whom none had been properly introduced.

"First, may I introduce Mr. Smith, to those of you who have not had the pleasure? I would like to add he also represents the U.S. Justice Department and is a Special Liaison to Homeland Security," I said solemnly.

"I understand his presence here now, but why was he involved so early on?" asked Linda.

"Because of the earlier murder of wealthy American citizens, he was also trying to understand Stormy's position, if any, in the affair," I explained.

"Everyone here understands that Stormy's scorned, wannabe lover hatched his diabolical plan to kill Stormy for revenge and hide his involvement among all the other murders." said Linda.

"And, when that failed, he tried to kill her himself; we all know how that ended," added Sterling.

"Yes, and with the motive discovered and the perpetrator revealed and deceased, I erroneously concluded the matter closed," said I.

"Yet it was not?" inquired Mike.

"Obviously not," joined Sterling. "But who would gain from her death now?"

"No one?" said Stormy hopefully.

"True, Stormy. No one would benefit from your death at this time," I agreed.

"But then, why kidnap me?" she asked.

"To make sure your death would be timely," I answered.

"What?" almost everyone in the room voiced simultaneously.

"Now you imply that someone does want to kill me?" asked a puzzled Stormy. "But you said ..."

"I meant that your death had to be engineered to occur at the right time, not sooner or later."

"What time is that?" she choked out.

"In your case, it would be after the repeal of the estate tax laws became effective, but before your nephews went broke," I explained.

"What?" she cried

"That way, your nephews could inherit twice as much money just when they needed it most," I continued. "They were not solvent and not willing to wait for your natural death, nor were they willing to pass up the biggest tax break ever to be enacted."

"You mean those two kidnappers were going to kill her only as soon as the time was right?" asked Linda.

CHAPTER SIXTY-THREE

MOST OF THE GROUP GASPED AND STORMY just sat mute. Finally, she placed her head in her hands and began crying softly.

I took Stormy back to the bedroom suite we were sharing at *Villa Mar.* We sat on the couch and she silently held on to me for a time.

"It will take a little while for me to digest all of this," she said. She rose and kissed me lightly on my mouth. "I need to thank you and yet I need some time to think and also some sleep," she said.

I asked the housekeeper to help her get ready for bed and handed her a sleeping pill to give Stormy.

"I am going to let you sleep now, but I'll be in the room next door if you need me. If not before, I'll meet you in the morning for breakfast when you're ready."

I closed the door behind me as I left the room. For the first time I felt secure about Stormy's safety.

CHAPTER SIXTY-FOUR

I RETURNED TO THE GREAT ROOM AND FOUND the group actively engaged in a discussion of the affair.

Mr. Smith from the Justice Department was explaining how easy it had been to get Tom and John to turn states' evidence and agree to testify before an upcoming federal grand jury, as well as both a House and Senate subcommittee.

They had both agreed to plead to one count of manslaughter each in return for their complete cooperation.

"Why would you need them to cooperate?" Sterling asked Smith. "You had them for the kidnapping of Stormy."

"True, but Stormy would have had a difficult time testifying that they were the ones who kidnapped her, because she was drugged the entire time they were in her presence. And the two orderlies that were let go have vanished and were not very credible anyway" responded Mr. Smith.

"But who did they kill, I mean if they are pleading to a manslaughter charge they must have killed someone?" asked Linda.

"You're correct, they killed the first shooter that tried to kill Stormy at the Garden Club reception," he answered.

"But you don't have any witnesses to that, do you?" continued Linda.

"Correct again," replied Smith. "Only their admission to the killing, which they bargained for to avoid any other possible charges."

"You see," he continued, "they were protecting Stormy so she would not die before the new law went into effect, and they kidnapped her so they could kill her at the right time. However, they never tried to kill her, so there was no attempted murder."

"Why didn't they kill Stormy and dispose of her along with the rest of the ones at the clinic?" pressed Linda.

"She didn't have the proper papers to be in the country, much less to be declared dead and cremated. Tom and John smuggled her in using a French passport and a phony name," replied Smith.

"Their plan was to smuggle her back into the states and arrange an accident for her after the repeal of the *Death Tax*." Smith continued.

"How were they going to get her back to the states?" asked Linda.

"They admitted they hadn't figured that out yet; but they were not concerned about finding a way."

"That's still letting them off awfully easy, in my opinion," said Linda, who refused to understand why it was necessary to bargain with criminals.

"They are not actually getting off. True, they are getting reduced sentences, but their testimony before Congress will be compelling, to say the least.

"What about the doctor?" Linda asked.

"Stormy never saw the Doctor," he replied.

"And, before you ask," continued Smith, "we are not going to prosecute the doctor. He will have his license to practice medicine revoked and will testify against the family members who conspired to defraud the government. The doctor," explained Smith, as Linda's mouth opened to object, "never harmed anyone. He was not a willing participant in Stormy's kidnapping and all of his charges were already clinically dead when placed into his care."

I added, "It is not illegal to try silly methods of preserving bodies, freezing or whatever, for the purpose of trying to resurrect them at a later date. His crime involved only fraud, since he had no intention of ever trying to bring them back."

"Correct," said Smith. "His only crime was to conspire with the relatives of the deceased to commit tax fraud, by hiding the victims' true time of death and signing phony death certificates after the *Death Tax* was repealed."

"Wouldn't the authorities be able to tell from an autopsy or something?" Linda asked.

"Perhaps, if the authorities found a reason to step in," Smith explained. "But there was a good chance that no one would find out. The deceased were all to be cremated, to remove any evidence. But they could not be cremated before they died—officially, that is—in order to accomplish the fraud. The doctor's certification of their time of death had to align with their cremation," explained Smith.

"The bodies had to arrive at the crematorium shortly after their declared death, as set out in the death certificate. The bodies would not be examined before cremation—just their papers—and there had to actually be a body to cremate," I added, "to make the time of death records appear legitimate."

"Think about it," interrupted Karl. "If you could inherit 600 million from old Aunt Daisy instead of 300 million, wouldn't it be more profitable and timely for her to die a little after she actually died.

With that, everyone left, simmering with their own thoughts and opinions.

CHAPTER SIXTY-FIVE

THE NEXT MORNING, AT *VILLA MAR*, WE ALL met for breakfast before going our separate ways. It was a warm comfortable gathering with our friends who we would not see again for a while.

Stormy and I wanted to sever all connection with the mad world that embroiled us in such insanity, at least for a while.

We flew back to Elizabeth Isle and boarded *Sea Witch* for an extended cruise round the Horn and on to the land down under. The gentle rolls of the big ocean swells had the effect of making the horizon disappear and reappear, time and again. The assured repetition of sky and water over and over induced an almost hypnotic state of relaxation.

We lay facing each other, on a double reclining chaise lounge on the aft deck. We were in our swimsuits; mine, just a simple pair of shorts, and Stormy in a white bikini that accented her curvaceous figure and smooth, silkily tanned skin.

We were being warmed by the late afternoon sun, which was dispersed by a high cirrus cloud cover, and cooled by the breeze generated by *Sea Witch* as she moved through the cold waters of the South Atlantic.

I rolled over on my back and Stormy moved closer to me.

She rested on her elbow and played her fingers through the hair on my chest.

"If you have any unanswered questions about this recent lunacy, ask them now or forever hold your tongue. If not, then I want to put this whole episode to rest and you to bed."

"Promise?" she teased.

"Promise!" I guaranteed.

"In that case, no further questions."

EPILOGUE

WHILE ROSS AND STORMY LANGUISHED AT the bottom of the world, the top half spun into a media frenzy. When the story broke about the thirty-one embalmed corpses found in an abandoned clinic in the Alps, it became the lead story for weeks.

All of the bodies were easily identified; each, in fact, had its own medical chart replete with names and exacting details of their disease or trauma that led to their transportation to the clinic. They had all died between four months and two weeks prior to being delivered to the clinic.

However, not a single one of them had ever been pronounced dead.

Generally, it requires a licensed physician, coroner, or in some cases a magistrate, to officially pronounce death. Without such a pronouncement and no obvious corpse lying about, the person presumably remains alive—at least on the books.

And that, of course, was what the conspiracy was all about. The doctor turned states' witness and testified that their deaths were planned to be "pronounced" after the favorable tax laws became effective.

No heirs sought to harm their benefactors before the

change in the tax law became effective. Once they realized that some nuts were randomly killing their benefactors-to-be, many heirs hired Karl and others to protect the benefactors from being killed before the law changed. Stormy's nephews did not want any harm to come to her before the change, and so the nephews paid for Karl, Tom, and John to protect her. In her case, however, the protection was to end with the repeal of the *Death Tax* and afterwards Tom and John were to arrange for her timely death, which was to take the form of an accident in the states. The *Death Tax* would have been repealed and the nephews would get double the amount they would otherwise have inherited from Stormy. The nephews were running out of time before their creditors would take over and had to work very hard at keeping the creditors at bay until the law change, but the reward for waiting just a little longer would have been worth the effort.

That story might have died down. In an everyday world, the UHNWIs (ultra high net worth individuals) are like overhead power lines—they are always there but seldom noticed. But when the Justice Department announced the indictments of more than a few heirs-to-be of conspiracy to commit tax fraud to the tune of billions and billions of dollars, the media pounced once again.

The general public, which does not like to be reminded of its sorry state of affairs, had its collective noses rubbed in it once more.

The talking heads took over. Daytime TV reeked of stories and anecdotal tales of horrors associated with sordid and greedy people.

Dollar amounts high enough to seduce the morally weak were also debated. The UHIWI's got the worst treatment from the talk shows. They pointed out that under the new tax law a trillion dollars could bypass the coffers of the public treasury.

The hottest debate centered on the effect of passing on such enormous wealth without regard to worthiness. Some argued this great inherited unearned wealth created not only an aristocracy, but an aristocracy of mediocrity.

However, no one said that you could not unplug granny's life support to give her a "timely death".